The Clinic

Venkit S. Iyer

Copyright © 2022 Venkit S. Iyer
All rights reserved
First Edition

PAGE PUBLISHING
Conneaut Lake, PA

First originally published by Page Publishing 2022

This book is a work of fiction. However, this fiction is based on facts and science. Names and events are added to make it readable as a story. Such names and events are imaginary even though they may have some resemblances to recent news. It is not meant to implicate any individual or organizations. Some of the actions described are purely unrealistic and nonexistent, while some other events are based on current developments in medical technology. It is up to the readers to make best sense out of the narratives. It is meant for enjoyment of reading and for promoting some thoughts in the process.

ISBN 978-1-6624-6741-7 (pbk)
ISBN 978-1-6624-6742-4 (digital)
LOC copyright registration number—Txu 002310565

Printed in the United States of America

Acknowledgments

I am thankful to Page Publishing, Inc. Conneaut, Pennsylvania, and their entire staff for helping me publish this book. Their help has been invaluable.

I am also thankful to Dr. Kedambadi P. Sheka for giving me valuable suggestions after proofreading the initial manuscript as well as the subsequent revision.

I am also thankful to Dr. M. P. Ravindra Nathan, Dr. Nathan Visweshwar, and Dr. Rajkumar Warrier for reviewing the final manuscript and giving me helpful suggestions.

I thank many of my friends and family for supporting me and encouraging me with helpful hints and opinions at various stages.

Endorsements

The Clinic is a fascinating and engaging novel that shines a light on the complex topic of genetic technology to treat a variety of medical disorders with illustrative cases that are at once informative and heartwarming. Although a fiction, the stories that you will read are based on scientific facts. The book unravels some of the critical breakthroughs in modern medicine. Gene therapy, by altering the very essence of our DNA coding, can be used for anything from fertility management and creating designer babies to behavior modification and even delaying the aging process. Looks like genes may be our destiny. Written in skillful conversational style by a master storyteller, this book is a must read for everyone.

—M. P. Ravindra Nathan, MD, FACC, FACP,
FRCP (London and Canada), FAHA
Cardiologist and author of *Stories from My Heart*
and *Second Chance: A Sister's Act of Love*
Emeritus editor of AAPI Journal

The third book from Dr. Venkit Iyer is informative and educational for an audience curious to explore new frontiers of science. It touches on technological advancement and also delves into human wants, needs, and emotions—an integral part of being human. Because of the nature of the subject, some knowledge of medical terminology is necessary to fully appreciate the nuances in this book. Being a physician with personal and professional encounters with the issues addressed in this book, I enjoyed reading this book. I congratulate Dr. Iyer for taking on a difficult subject in a conversational manner and is likely to be palatable to most readers. What we think impossible now may become routine for the next generation. This book is timely—touching on the mRNA vaccine for COVID-19, making use of advancements in genetic technology. This book has two parts: one dealing with medical and the other with cybercrime and associated new challenges the world is facing. I am sure Dr. Iyer has more tricks in his bag to keep one's curiosity growing. Kudos for tackling a difficult topic in as a fictional chronicle!

—Rajkumar K. Warrier, MD, FACP
Gastroenterologist

Recent progress in the medical field has been at breakneck speed. I am specifically referring to research in the area of genetics. Society may not be able to keep abreast of the developments that could lead to Frankenstein-type mad scientists. Dr. Venkit Iyer is wisely warning us about the double-edged sword of genetic research. We need to be careful in monitoring and controlling genetic research for the safety of us all.

—Kedambadi P. Sheka, MD, FACS
Retired thoracic and cardiovascular surgeon

Contents

Preface 9
Chapter 1: The Destiny 13
Chapter 2: The Clinic 28
Chapter 3: The Process 45
Chapter 4: The Surrogate 49
Chapter 5: The Bank 58
Chapter 6: The Gene Test 66
Chapter 7: The Laboratory 70
Chapter 8: The Website 83
Chapter 9: The Travel 92
Chapter 10: The Creation 95
Chapter 11: The Disorders 99
Chapter 12: The Gender 105
Chapter 13: The Parent 111
Chapter 14: The Cloned 119
Chapter 15: The Stem Cell 125
Chapter 16: The Sequencing 129
Chapter 17: The Editing 133
Chapter 18: The Harvesting 141
Chapter 19: The Transformations 149
Chapter 20: The Services 152
Chapter 21: The Money 158
Chapter 22: The Recruitment 161
Chapter 23: The Procurement 166
Chapter 24: The Progress 170
Chapter 25: The Delivery 175
Chapter 26: The Raid 182
Books Written by the Author 193

Preface

This book is for mature and informed readers, since it deals with genetics and reproductive technology. It is a fiction. However, this fiction is based on facts and science. What we considered as fiction in the past is normal everyday reality today. Medical technology keeps advancing steadily and is looking toward reaching goals that were unthinkable a few years ago. Not only do people want to live longer and healthier, but they also want their children to have a better life. Some of these efforts will be made by genetic manipulations, sometimes inside the uterus, before a child is born, to make them smarter, taller, and stronger.

Futuristic fertility clinic will do more than just give advice on pregnancy or help with in vitro or in vivo fertilization. They will have integral collaboration with genetic laboratories, which can detect and cure congenital disorders before the children are born. Not only mothers will have the ability of having a child; they will also have a choice on gender, color, IQ, longevity, and physical power. The futuristic woman will have the ability to custom-create her newborn, irrespective of the parents' features or qualities.

The world will respect women as the most needed gender to carry the human race forward, since they have the necessary reproductive organs with them. They have the breast milk and hormones, right temperament, and desire to nurture and raise the baby. Men have only the sperms to offer, but those sperms can be obtained from a bank or from any man of her choice, not necessarily by sex alone. If sperms are not available, she can have them made out of her own cells such as skin or muscles. A woman can clone herself, whereas a man will still need a live uterus to incubate the baby. Genetic laboratories will be equipped to meet the new challenges.

Also, women can decide when and how they want to get pregnant based on their career situations and personal choices. She can have her eggs frozen and used for fertilization whenever she is ready. There will be no rush to become a mother until she finishes her education and career goals. The lab can freeze ovum or eggs, sperms, and other tissues for indefinite time periods and activate them as needed.

In order to connect the fertility clinic and the genetic laboratory, it will be necessary to use a dark website. Such a website will facilitate other activities of interest to its members, along with the genetic research and treatment. High degree of privacy and secrecy will be maintained. World Genetic Research Laboratory is engaged in advanced research in creating life, prolonging life, treating diseases, eradicating congenital disorders, discovering newer transplantation procedures, and finding new surgical techniques. The secretive World Genetic Research Laboratory has the ability to conduct live human experimentations, genetic manipulations, along with use of new medications and surgical measures.

Most countries do not allow this type of work on their land due to moral, ethical, and legal concerns. However, there is a need and a desire to have this type of research and facility. The benefit is that congenital disorders can be corrected before the children are born, hereditary disorders can be eliminated, and children can be made to live healthier and smarter. Longevity of human race will be increased. Medical science will advance. Cancers and degenerative disorders will be cured. Transplantation techniques will be improved. Live human experimentation will enhance traditional time-consuming clinical trials. The bad side is the unknown side effects and complications that can occur when meddling with nature. Mutants can be born with unknown qualities and behavior. These offspring will have to be studied for a lifetime and compared with regular humans. Moral and ethical concerns, including sacrifice of other humans, would be a great concern.

However, medical science must advance. Progress must go on. Scientists have the thirst and eagerness to explore the unknown. They want to experiment and discover. People with financial resources want to get things done now and not later. But no one wants to be dirtying his or her own hands. The World Genetic Research Laboratory, World Fertility and Genetic Clinic, and Dark Web Site work together and wield much power on the future of humanity. The world needs them, but the world is also afraid of them.

Fictitious names used in the book

Three institutions, namely World Fertility and Genetic Clinic, World Genetic Research Laboratory, and Dark Web Site work together.

Their work involves helping with fertility and genetic counseling to general public. This is the frontline business. The back business is conducting major advanced research in genetic technology and transplantation techniques. The Dark Web Site connects the two to conduct business that sometimes involves immoral activities.

Clients at the clinic

Rani and Sooraj—a couple who are unable to conceive after five years of marriage

Melinda and Linda—lesbian women who want to have their own natural-born child without participation by a man

David and Susan Lindsey—wants to have artificial insemination from the husband who was declared brain-dead following an automobile accident

Melissa Winslow—wants in-vitro fertilization due to aging issues and prior miscarriage

Rena Kaur—needs in-vitro fertilization due to medical problems

Razia Begum—wants a child at any cost without the participation of her husband, who is threatening divorce or a second marriage, blaming her for the barren state

Karen Dran—needs a surrogate mother due to prior hysterectomy but had functioning ovaries left in place

Clients at the bank

Karen Wheeler—career woman who has no time to have a family now. She wants to freeze her eggs now so she can have her baby when she is ready.

John Edwards—student at Yale University who wants to donate sperms for money

Clients at the World Genetic Research Laboratory

Parsuram and Jyothy—a couple who want to have a son at any cost. They already have four daughters.

Nora Gerber and Don Gerber—a couple who have a fetus diagnosed to have Down syndrome by gene testing and want to have it corrected before birth

Nicki and John Pappas—a couple who have a fetus diagnosed to have Thalassemia and want to have it corrected before birth by gene therapy

Chapter 1

The Destiny

Rani and Sooraj had a grand wedding in Gujarat, India, six years ago. He was a computer science graduate, and she had a master's degree in home science. He was working for a multinational company near Mumbai, and she was working for a hotel as a hospitality agent.

A mutual family friend told them:

"Just meet each other and tell us what you think. It is time for you guys to get married. Before you know, you will be too old."

Their parents also repeated:

"We think it will be a good alliance. They are a respectable family. They have college degrees. Don't say no unless you have a reason."

So they met on a prearranged date. There was opportunity for them to talk to each other. They did not find any reason to reject the proposal. So they agreed with their parents to go along with the wedding.

It was a well-planned arranged marriage with permission and blessings from parents on both sides. Everyone agreed it was a good alliance. There was a great deal of excitement and enthusiasm on both sides. The groom arrived on a white horse, wearing a red turban. The bride arrived in the company of her many friends, wearing a gold-laced glittering red sari. Over three hundred guests attended the gala event. The food was great. Dinner and dancing were magnificent.

The first year of their married life in Mumbai was honeymoon period. There was a lot of partying, sightseeing, and traveling. They wanted to postpone any childbirth or pregnancy. They wanted to enjoy the time together, to get to know each other, and were taking all precautions possible. Setting up the new apartment, buying kitchen utensils and essential household items, buying a television set and furniture were all time-consuming but engaging activities.

They were saying, "Let us wait for a year or two before we have a family. We have plenty of time."

Surprise and joy came out of the blue when Sooraj's boss called him to his office one day.

"Hi, Sooraj. How are you doing?"

"I am doing okay, sir. Is there anything wrong?"

"Nothing wrong. I have some good news for you."

"What happened, sir?"

"Well, you are the lucky winner. You have a chance to go to the US if you want to."

"Sir!"

"The head office in the US wants to offer you a chance to work in California on a new project."

Sooraj looked happy with a smile on his face.

"They would sponsor you for an H-1B visa, and your wife will be able to go with you."

"How did they select me, sir?"

"It looks like they are short of hands over there. They were looking for experienced candidates from within the company, and your name came up."

"How about travel, accommodation, and salary?"

"You will be making ten times more money than what you are getting now. They would provide a salary comparable to American workers at that level. They would pay for economy-class plane ticket for you and your wife. I am told they will help you find a modest accommodation in the vicinity of the workplace."

Sooraj could not hold in his joy. He was almost bursting.

"How much time do I have, sir?"

"We must know an answer within one week whether you are accepting it or not. If all the paperwork is in order, you will be leaving within the next two months."

THE CLINIC

"Thank you very much, sir. I shall talk it over with my family and tell you tomorrow, sir."

Everyone was glad to hear the news. Both parents got jubilant. They calculated the salary by converting it to Indian rupees. Rani's mother claimed that it was the good-luck stars of her daughter that brought this good news.

"I knew it from her horoscope. She has a fortune with the stars on her favor. It indicated that she will bring good luck to her husband."

So Rani and Sooraj were busy for the next two months, getting things ready for the travel. They had to get the passports and visa.

"I have to stitch a new suit to look decent."

"I, too, need to buy new clothes to look modern."

The visit to the US consulate in Mumbai was chore, which took two days of intense interviews and questioning. Finally, all the paperwork was ready.

Travel by airplane was a first-time experience for both of them. They had never gone outside India at any time. It was a memorable journey, and they were thoroughly surprised with the courtesy and service of "air hostesses."

Finally, they arrived in California. Everything was new and exciting. Roads were clean and uncluttered compared to Mumbai. It was quite nice inside the small, furnished rental apartment. There were so many new things, so many different appliances, and so many new issues they had to address. It was a lot of fun and excitement. Another year went by before they knew it.

Rani was talking to her mother on WhatsApp using her cell phone, describing all the various exciting new lifestyle in America. That was when her mother made a first hint.

"How is your health? Are you doing okay?"

"Yes, Mom. Why are you asking?"

"Nothing special. Just wondering."

They bought a small used car and went for random driving. They visited Disney World one weekend. They made a few Indian friends and visited an Indian grocery store. Time went by quickly. Sooraj had applied for immigration visa through his company. He was doing a good job at the workplace, and they were willing to sponsor him for the green card.

Another year had slipped by. Slowly the desire to have a child was sinking in. Rani stopped taking the birth control pills.

Sooraj was talking to his mother on FaceTime one evening after work. She was a bit more blunt.

"It is three years since you got married. We are waiting to see if we can get a grandchild soon."

"Mom, we are still young, and there is time."

"You are not that young anymore. You are going to be thirty, and Rani is going to be twenty-nine. I had two children by age twenty-two."

He did not say anything. Rani was listening to the conversation. She was also quiet. They touched each other and held hands for a long time.

"We are going to have to try. Don't work late, exercise a little more, and let us go to bed early."

She cooked delicious food and wore nice dress to greet him from work. She took vitamins and some food supplements. He started reading books to increase fertility. He exercised more and showered at night. They went to the Hindu temple in California and conducted a special prayer and devotional ceremony for good luck. Months went by with no changes in her cycles.

They had several good friends by this time, and Rani started talking to them about tips for getting pregnant.

"I would suggest you should see your family doctor for a consultation and a medical checkup," said one friend.

Another one said, "I have heard about a good fertility clinic. It is called World Fertility and Genetic Clinic. You may want to check it out."

One of her neighbors was Razia Begum, who was having similar issues, and they started comparing notes. She confided that she had overheard a conversation between her husband and her mother-in-law.

THE CLINIC

"After four years of marriage, you have no children. What are you going to do about it? I was hoping to see a grandchild before I close my eyes and say goodbye to this world."

The husband replied, "Mom, we have been trying hard. It just does not seem to click."

"Maybe it is time for you to think about a second wife. I shall talk to the Mullah. We can find out the best option, whether to divorce her or not."

Her husband was willing to consider a second marriage at the behest of his mother. Razia started to feel pressure and stress. That was when Razia Begum decided to have a private consultation at the fertility clinic, since her husband refused to have a medical checkup.

In certain parts of the world, married women without children are put down and insulted by the family. A barren woman is considered a bad omen and a cursed person. The fault may be with the male, but it is blamed on the woman to the extent she has to find a way of getting pregnant to save face. It can lead to second marriage of the husband with or without a divorce.

Rani started feeling pressure hearing her story. She started doubting herself and started doubting her husband. Could there be a problem? Should they go for a medical consultation? They started having some discussions that went nowhere. Should they see their regular family physician or should they go to a fertility clinic? After some discussions, they decided to go for a routine medical checkup with the family doctor who was assigned to them through the medical insurance at the workplace.

The doctor was a middle-aged lady.

After signing in and checking their insurance card, they were asked to fill out several pages of forms for a first-visit patient.

The nurse interviewed them first before taking Rani into an examination room.

"Do you have any medical problems?"

"No, we are here for a regular checkup."

"When was your last medical checkup?"

"We came from India two years ago. We had no reason to go for any checkup. Before they issued the visa to come here, there was a medical clearance from a doctor over there. We were married for nearly a year by then."

"So this is your first visit to any doctor here in California?"

"Yes."

She took their height, weight, temperature, and blood pressure.

"Do you take any medications?"

"I take some vitamins. I used to take birth control pills, but I have stopped them over a year ago."

She made some notations on the chart and closed the door.

"The doctor will be in soon."

After about ten minutes of waiting, the doctor walked in with a smile on her face.

"So you are here for a first-visit routine medical checkup as my nurse says?"

"Yes, doctor."

"You have been in good health all along?"

"Yes, doctor."

"You have had all the childhood vaccinations, I assume."

"Yes, doctor."

"Do you have any problems that you want to talk to me?"

"Well, we have been married for three years now. We are trying to have a baby."

"You were on birth control pills up until last year, I notice."

"Yes, doctor. First, we thought we would wait for a year. Then we moved to California from India. We needed some time. Now for the past one year, we have been trying."

"Okay, let me examine both of you separately."

They were asked to go behind the curtain and wear the paper gown after undressing. The doctor made a complete physical examination of both of them, washed her hands, and told them to get dressed.

"I shall talk to you in the office." Then she walked out to see another patient next room.

Rani and Sooraj got dressed and sat in her office.

The doctor walked in.

"Well, I do not see anything abnormal in either of you. That should be good news. We shall do some blood tests, urine test, and thyroid function tests. I shall call you if anything is abnormal in these tests. In the meantime, just stay well, eat good food, exercise, relax, do not drink alcohol, and sleep well. Let us see what happens in next few cycles. The best time for fertility is in the mid cycle of your periods. That is when the ovum is released, and it remains good but for only four days."

"Doctor, are there any tips you can give us to increase chance of fertility by natural means?"

"Certain measures are useful. Eat a healthy diet, exercise well, sleep good, reduce stress, and find happiness and love."

"What type of diet would you recommend for us?"

"Your diet should contain adequate amounts of antioxidants in the form of fresh fruits, berries, and vegetables. Use less trans fats and less of carbohydrates, more of fiber and omega-3 fatty acids. Avoid obesity."

"Anything else?"

"Avoid alcohol and smoking."

"Should we take vitamins?"

"You could take vitamin E, D, zinc, fish oil, or just multivitamins available over the counter."

"Should we be taking any prescription medicines to increase fertility?"

"There are certain medications available. But before I go there, it would be a good idea to try these natural methods. Then if necessary, we can consult a gynecologist for you and a urologist for your husband. At that point, we can consider fertility medicines for both of you if necessary."

They went home happy knowing that there is nothing wrong with them. They conveyed the news of good medical checkup to their mothers in the evening. She started counting the days in her cycles, marking the best days on her calendar. They instituted those measures recommended by the doctor.

Six months passed by, and nothing much changed.

Pressure was building up internally and from both families. Even some friends started oblique questions like "How long you have been married?" or "Do you have any children?" or "Enjoy now, once you have children, it will be a lot of new problems."

They called their family doctor and requested referral to the gynecologist for her and for the urologist for him. They wanted to be sure and were ready to obtain prescription drugs to increase fertility. They went to meet these specialists separately on different days.

The gynecologist's office was in a medical arts building next to a hospital, and it appeared to be a group practice. After the usual checking-in rituals and nurse's interrogation, the doctor walked in. She was a pleasant lady of second-generation Indian origin by the name of Meena.

"So you are here to talk about fertility issues, as I understand from your primary care doctor?"

"Yes, doctor. We have been trying now almost three and a half years after our marriage."

"What have you done so far?"

"We followed instructions given by the family doctor, watching diet, doing exercises, taking vitamins, and following the cycle. My husband is also doing these things."

"Very good. I am going to do a complete GYN examination, and afterward we shall also do a pelvic ultrasound. I have results of your blood tests and other lab tests sent to us from your family doctor's office."

"Okay, doctor."

The doctor did a complete examination of her pelvis and abdomen. As she left, an ultrasound technician wheeled in her machine to do a portable bedside ultrasound of her pelvis. Rani tried to ask questions to the technician as to the findings.

She just smiled and said, "The doctor will talk to you."

She got dressed and was seated in the consultation room. Dr. Meena walked in and started explaining.

"Actually, I do not see anything that is abnormal. All your organs, uterus, tubes, and ovaries look normal on the ultrasound.

The pelvic examination is also normal, and all your lab tests are also normal."

"What causes infertility in women?"

"There are many reasons. Sometimes it is genetic abnormalities. It can be due to hormonal issues. Some people have abnormal mucous or obstructive pathways in their genital tract. Common problem nowadays is postponement of pregnancy to a later age due to socioeconomic reasons."

"So what shall I do, doctor?"

"I can prescribe certain medications that will increase the ovarian function. The first line of medicine is called clomiphene citrate, known commonly as Clomid. It stimulates your pituitary gland to release more of two other hormones called follicular stimulating hormone (FSH) and luteinizing hormone (LH). These hormones in turn will stimulate your ovarian follicle to make and release ova more readily."

"Are there any side effects, doctor?"

"Some people feel discomfort in lower abdomen. There have been some instances of having twins."

"Are there other medicines and stronger ones?"

"Yes. Next, we try another medicine by name Letrozole (Femara). Still stronger are injections of gonadotropin. But the injections are reserved for special situations needing in-vitro fertilization. Estrogens can also help to improve female fertility."

"How do I know the time my ovulation is happening in my body?"

"Keep a strict calendar. Ovulation occurs ten to sixteen days before your period starts. You may feel the cervical mucous getting wetter. If you take your daily temperature, you may find that your temperature goes up by one degree during ovulation."

As she was getting ready to leave, she said, "I have asked the nurse to give you a couple of videos on sex and fertility information. You and your husband can watch it. It contains educational materials."

"Okay."

"Also, we shall wait to hear from the urologist on the status of your husband, and then we shall go from there."

Sooraj returned from his visit with the urologist. Rani was curious to know how it went. She told him all about her trip to the gynecologist and the prescription for a fertility drug. She also told him about the video they were going watch together at night.

Sooraj went over his details. The physical examination went well.

He was told that certain conditions would reduce sperm count in men. They are varicocele, undescended testicles, and obstruction to vas deference, retrograde ejaculation, erectile dysfunctions, anti-sperm antibodies, childhood surgery for hernia or hydrocele, and some unknown reasons. He did not have any of those things. Then they wanted to have a semen analysis, which also came back as normal. He, too, felt good having gotten a clean report.

Three months later, she missed her periods! She was surprised and wanted to be sure. She went to the local pharmacy and got the pregnancy test kit and checked her urine. Yes, it was positive! She tested it for two more days to make sure it was true. She was all smiles when Sooraj returned from work that day. After dinner, she broke the news to him. He was thrilled to hear.

"Are you sure? Did you do the urine test? Wow."

"Yes, I think we are good."

"Are you going to call your mom?"

"I think I will wait for couple of weeks."

"Do we need to go and see the gynecology doctor?"

"Yes, I think we should and set up an appointment with Dr. Meena. She should know."

"Okay, go ahead and call their office and make an appointment to see her soon."

"You need to be careful. Don't do any heavy work."

They both wished they were in India at this time with their families who would be overjoyed, celebrating, and helping her with her daily chores.

THE CLINIC

In the morning, Rani called Dr. Meena's office to give them the good news and to set up an appointment to see her as soon as possible. The nurse came on the line and interrogated her.

"So when was your last period?"

"It was six weeks ago. I skipped this month's by two weeks now."

"Did you test it with urine stick?"

"Yes, I did it on two separate days. Both days it came back as positive. So when do I come to see the doctor?"

"There is no rush. Our next elective prenatal appointment is four weeks from now. That should be a good time, and we would do an ultrasound at the same time."

So Rani made the appointment and hung up the phone. She was all excited and did not know what else to do. She went for grocery shopping to cook some great Indian masala food with roti.

Three weeks later, all of a sudden, she experienced severe pain in the lower abdomen and pelvis, as if something was tearing apart inside her body. She called Dr. Meena's office and wanted to have a checkup right away. The nurse came on the line and sort of reassured her that these symptoms happen for some people. She was to call again if she noticed any vaginal bleeding.

The following day, the pain continued but as a dull ache. That afternoon, she noticed a sizable vaginal bleeding. Again, she called the doctor's office. This time, they told her to get there immediately.

They did a blood test for pregnancy, which came back as positive. Then they did an ultrasound of the pelvis to evaluate the fetus in the uterus. However, the fetus could not be found in the uterus or anywhere else. Vaginal bleeding continued. The doctor came over and evaluated everything.

The doctor told her, "I think you had an ectopic pregnancy. Some people call it tubal pregnancy. That is why your pregnancy test is positive, but we cannot find the fetus in the expected place in the uterus. With your symptoms, it appears that your body is trying to expel it spontaneously."

"Oh my god."

"Your abdomen is soft, and the vital signs and blood counts are normal. I am going to prescribe a medication called methotrexate to complete the evacuation of the fetus. It is an injection given into your arm."

The nurse administered the injection while she was lying in bed.

There was more bleeding, and a glob of clot also came out. An hour later, the pain subsided. After observing her vital signs for another four hours, they allowed her to go home and rest.

Sooraj was with her during this entire time. Both of them realized that she had a miscarriage. It could have been more dangerous than what had occurred. They were depressed with the loss of pregnancy but also relieved to know that she was safe. She was to rest at home, watch for any more abdominal pain or vaginal bleeding, avoid strenuous activities, and avoid sex. She was also to return to the office for another checkup and blood test after three weeks to ensure that the pregnancy was gone completely.

Three weeks later, as per appointment, she went back to Dr. Meena's office. True enough, the blood test at this time showed the pregnancy hormone level was much lower than the earlier test. She had no symptoms and she felt normal.

Next few weeks were one of depression and soul-searching for both Rani and Sooraj. What did we do wrong? Why me? Could we have done anything different? There were some mild hormone-related changes in her body with breast engorgement and nausea. She felt elated on the prospect of motherhood and felt saddened on the loss of opportunity. She cried a little. Talking about this with their parents and friends was more painful. They started doing their own research on the causes of ectopic pregnancy, symptoms, and treatment. She went to the local library, and he did his search on his laptop.

They learned a lot about pregnancy and ectopic pregnancy. Normally the fertilization takes place inside the fallopian tube, and then the blastomere slowly glides down into the uterus, where it gets attached to its wall and then the fetus grows. In ectopic pregnancy, the fertilized blastomere is not inside the uterus but somewhere outside of it. Most of the ectopic pregnancy, nearly 90 percent of them are inside the fallopian tube itself where the initial fertilization takes place. It is stuck there, unable to migrate down to the uterus. Sometimes it can be in the abdominal cavity, in the vicinity of pelvic organs. Initial symptoms are nausea, pelvic pain and vaginal bleeding, or shoulder pain. Only 50 percent of patients notice any symptoms initially. Sometimes it can burst through the fallopian tube and can cause massive intra-abdominal bleeding necessitating emergency open surgery.

They asked Dr. Meena, "What causes one to get ectopic pregnancy?"

"Common causes are previous pelvic inflammatory disease, prior pelvic surgery, and sexually transmitted diseases, endometriosis, use of certain drugs, including birth control pills and smoking. Previous ectopic pregnancy is a warning sign that it can happen again."

"How is it diagnosed?"

"Diagnosis is by high levels of human chorionic gonadotropic hormone (HCG) while the sonogram, especially trans vaginal sonogram (TVS), showing the fetus is not in the uterus but elsewhere."

"How is it treated?"

"If the ectopic pregnancy is diagnosed early, it can be treated with methotrexate (Trexal), which dissolves the blastomere inside the fallopian tube, and it goes away over three or four weeks. Sometimes laparoscopic surgery can be done to control the bleeding and ligate the fallopian tube without removing the ovaries. The worse scenario is when it becomes a life-threatening emergency with massive internal hemorrhage, needing emergency open surgery and ligation of that fallopian tube."

Four months went by resting and waiting. The desire for motherhood became stronger than ever. They followed all the instructions for better fertility. After getting a green signal from Dr. Meena, they decided to try it again. They went to the temple and made a special prayer and observed partial fasting on Mondays as a traditional tribute to the fertility goddess. She watched the calendar closely and chose the best days to be together for union again.

Good God, she missed her periods again by one week. Again, she checked the urine dipstick. Again, it was positive! They were elated and rechecked it for two more days. Again, they all came back positive! Two days later, she called Dr. Meena's office and talked to the nurse. Everyone was happy. Dr. Meena herself called her and warned her to be careful. Again, she reminded her of the possibility that ectopic pregnancy can happen again, since it happened once before. She was to watch for any symptoms and contact them immediately if any may occur. They decided to keep the pregnancy a secret and not to inform their parents or friends until after a couple of months.

Six weeks later, Rani became very sick all of a sudden. It happened like a lightning with severe searing pain in the right side of her pelvis, back pain, and vomiting. She almost fainted. Sooraj came rushing back from the office. He called Dr. Meena's office about the situation. The nurse told them to rush her to the office as quickly as possible.

Examination showed vaginal bleeding; HCG test was very high, and the ultrasound showed absent fetus in the uterus. But the bigger problem was that they noticed the presence of fluid in the pelvis behind the uterus, which suggested internal bleeding, and found a localized bulging in the right fallopian tube, all suggesting a rupture of the right fallopian tube from an ectopic pregnancy. Her blood pressure was normal, but her pulse rate was rapid.

Things moved very rapidly and then onward. They rushed her to the hospital close by and took her directly to the operating room. Dr. Meena advised them that she was in great danger of dying if immediate surgery is not performed. The ectopic pregnancy had made a rupture of the fallopian tube, and she was hemorrhaging internally. They would try a laparoscopic procedure, and if not successful, they would have to make a cut and open her abdomen. Consent forms were signed, and blood was sent for cross-matching. The whole situation was moving and turning very rapidly. Sooraj did not even have time to gather his thoughts. She just disappeared into the inner rooms and dark walls of the hospital. He just sat there in the waiting room, holding his breath.

About an hour later, Dr. Meena came out with a sigh of relief.

She said, "Everything went well. She is safe."

"We were able to do a laparoscopic procedure, also called keyhole surgery, thus avoiding a bigger open-cut surgery. We were able to stop the internal bleeding. She did have an ectopic pregnancy in the right fallopian tube, which had just burst through its wall."

At the end, she said, "Unfortunately we had to remove that segment of the fallopian tube by clipping it on either side and remove the blastomere along with the ruptured part of the tube. The ovaries are intact and good on both sides. The left fallopian tube looked normal but somewhat long and tortuous. The main thing is that she is out of danger and will be able to go home in one or two days. There is still hope for her to get pregnant in the future, but we shall talk about it at another time."

Two days later, Rani was brought home in a weak, tired, and listless fashion. She did not want to talk or eat. She just sat there staring at the wall. There was still mild vaginal bleeding. The surgery site was hurting but not too bad. She could get up and go to bathroom.

Sooraj took a day off, tried to cook some food, and encouraged her to eat something and go to bed. It was good that she did not say anything about this second attempt to her mother or mother-in-law. What were they going to say, anyway, other than make her feel worse? She felt pathetic and depressed.

Slowly, over the next several days, she got used to the situation. She slowly recovered. She had an appointment to see the nurse for wound checkup. It was healing well, and there were no sutures to remove. They made another appointment with Dr. Meena a few weeks later to discuss further steps.

Chapter 2

The Clinic

Rani had an appointment with Dr. Meena about six weeks after discharge. Sooraj accompanied her for a discussion. Doctor examined her and noted that she had fully recovered from surgery and the tiny wound had healed well. Now it was time to discuss future plans.

"You had a close call. We are happy that your life was not endangered. As you recall, I had mentioned that there was a high chance to have a second ectopic pregnancy since you had a previous ectopic."

"Yes, doctor. Where do we go from here?"

"We were forced to tie off your right fallopian tube since it was damaged and torn, but we did not damage that ovary. In fact, both your ovaries are functioning. Your other fallopian tube is still intact but somewhat tortuous and long. We have not caused any damage to it. Theoretically speaking, you can still become pregnant with one fallopian tube."

"Can I get another ectopic again in that tube also?"

"Yes, it is a good possibility. We do not know how it is functioning inside unless we do additional tests and x-rays."

"What do you suggest, doctor?"

"Actually, that is what I was going to talk about. My first suggestion is that you should consult a specialist physician to plan for an in-vitro fertilization"

"Why?"

"Because it would be a safer option for you. This way, you are no longer depending upon the fallopian tube's function. The fertilized blastomere is directly implanted inside the uterus."

"What is involved in this procedure?"

"First step is to have a consultation with the specialist. They may do additional tests and evaluations. Then your eggs are retrieved by a small surgical procedure. This egg is then fertilized with the sperm from your husband's body in the genetic laboratory. The actual fertilization takes place outside of your body. This fertilized blastomere is then implanted directly inside your uterus. Then the fetus grows, and in due course, you will deliver your own baby."

"Is this what they used to call test tube baby?"

"Yes. Only because the fertilization takes place in the laboratory and then it is implanted back. It may not be in a test tube, but it is a common way of expression."

"Are there other methods described?"

"Yes. One is called GIFT, which stands for Gamete Intra Fallopian Transfer. Another one is called ZIFT, which stands for Zygote Intra Fallopian Transfer. These are not commonly done and are not suitable for someone with fallopian tube problems."

"Is there some particular doctor you recommend?"

"The best place we recommend is a facility called World Fertility and Genetic Clinic in Los Angeles. I can give you a copy of your medical records, and you can call them to make your own appointment."

"We need some time to think things over."

"Yes. By all means, it is not an urgent issue. Take your time, read up on it, and talk it over with your friends and family."

"Okay, doctor."

"Wish you the best. Feel free to call us for any questions and concerns."

That was the end of the conversation. The doctor left the room to see another patient. Rani and Sooraj came home with a heavy heart and a lot of thinking.

There was a lot of soul-searching and web searching to do. They did not want to talk to their parents, who will only make them get more depressed. They also did not want to talk about the topic with their friends. However, they made certain indirect and oblique inquiries. She remembered that her neighbor Razia Begum had gone to World Fertility and Genetic Clinic in Los Angeles to become pregnant and wanted to know about the place. She talked to her privately about her experience.

Razia had only good things to say about the place. She went over her personal difficult decisions after demanding confidentiality.

Her problem was that she was normal and healthy, but the husband refused to get any kind of checkup in spite of being infertile. He was planning to get married to a second wife and divorce her in the meantime. She was adamant to get pregnant one way or another.

She said to herself, "Either I get pregnant or I get divorced. Pregnancy is the better choice for my life. As a divorcee, I will be thrown out in the streets."

So she decided to get artificial insemination from the sperm bank there without her husband's knowledge or permission. She chose a donor with similar ethnicity and complexion as that of her husband. Hurray. Success was achieved in two months. Once she announced her pregnancy, everyone in her family was overjoyed. She saved her own marriage and her standing in the family. She gave birth to a male child in nine months.

"What a cute baby! He looks just like his father," said her mother-in-law.

The baby was accepted and anointed as the next heir to all their wealth and properties. No divorce, no second marriage, and the secret remained a secret forever. The mother-in-law was thrilled. Her husband started staying home more often to cuddle the baby, and he would show it off to all visitors as a proud father!

Rani and Sooraj had some long discussions about various options. They were getting older; it was now nearly four and half years since they got married. He was going to be thirty-two, and she was thirty-one. They had to make decisions soon, as the time clock was running out.

They had thought about the option of adopting a baby if they could not have one of their own. They also talked it over with some friends. One day, they had a group discussion.

"But the adoption process is quite complicated, expensive, and legally regulated in the US."

"How often do they adopt a child in US?"

"Over one hundred thousand couples have been waiting to adopt a child while there is a dearth of adoptable babies."

"Would you be comfortable to raise an adopted child?"

"Depends to whom you ask the question. Some people find it as the best solution. Some others see the adopted child as another pet, just same as a dog or cat, with no actual emotional attachment. Some others do not like the idea at all."

"Why don't they like the idea?"

"In spite of all the hurdles, it will not be the same as having your own baby. No matter what, an adopted baby is still someone else's baby, either unwanted or abandoned. Why should we carry the burden of someone else's misdeeds or sins?"

"Have you heard of stories where the childless people have gone to extreme length as to steal a child?"

"Yes. These types of incidences have occurred. They had also heard stories about abducting or stealing newborn infants from the nursery of the hospital. All newborns look alike, and it is easy for someone pretending to be the mother, take the baby for breastfeeding, and disappear."

"Don't they have security measures to prevent such things from happening?"

"Many security measures are in place in the Western world. However, health care is very disorganized and lax in other parts of the world."

"Tell us about any unusual situations."

"They had heard of a story when the nurse in charge of the nursery helped a childless couple by selling a newborn baby from the maternity ward. The mother was a mentally challenged girl who was raped by a caregiver. She did not even know that she was pregnant and was taken to the hospital for vomiting. The nurse in charge felt it would be better for the child to be adopted immediately, and circumstances came together for her to steal and sell the baby. She told the mother that the baby was stillborn and had died. In any case, she was incapable of raising the child due to her mental deficiency."

They talked about women opting for abortions following casual sex and about the number of newborns being abandoned by mothers and left out as orphans. Some children are neglected or abused by their family. What is wrong with this society? On one side, people want a child of their own at any cost, and on the other side, people do not want to get pregnant at all or abandon a normal healthy child.

Rani and Sooraj wished to have a baby; they had tried hard and they were willing to go to any extent and meet any price just to be a parent.

Rani and Sooraj finally decided to get a consultation at the World Fertility and Genetic Clinic after long discussions, thoughts and after thoughts, arguments and disagreements, soul-searching, and hesitations. They said to themselves, "There is nothing to lose by having a consultation. Listen to what they have to say. Look over the facility and get an idea about their outfit."

They had seen the glaring billboard in big red color visible from the highway. They had seen the newspaper advertisement promising the best of best results, ending with a happy face. They had seen the enticing television advertisements showing a smiling mother cuddling a chubby baby. If at all possible, they wanted to have a baby of their own.

She asked Razia again, "How does this place look like?"

"World Fertility and Genetic Clinic is a freestanding large building on the side street with a large signboard visible from the main street. There is a guard at the gated front entrance to the compound. It has tall compound walls all around with security cameras covering the entire ground. Secrecy of the business and privacy of the customers are of paramount importance. Customers can park inside the compound without being noticed by pedestrians."

"Why are they so concerned about security?"

"Many strict measures are set up to maintain secrecy, privacy, and confidentiality of the clients. Criminal elements can use the information to blackmail VIPs or celebrities who would like to avoid unnecessary publicity in the social media."

THE CLINIC

"Do they have branches, or this is one-of-a-kind facility?"

"It is a franchise operation. Branches of the World Fertility and Genetic Clinic are present in every major city across the globe. Each clinic runs independently, complying with the local rules and regulations. But they are all linked together through a Dark Web Site (DWS) to exchange information, auction the products, transfer collected materials, and conduct research using the World Genetic Research Laboratory. In addition, they have links and business arrangements with numerous other fertility clinics in various towns."

"I assume you need to make a prior appointment."

"Yes. Patients are seen by appointment only, and they are pre-screened with a questionnaire filled out online. It is a very detailed questionnaire, wanting to know all the medical, social, psychological, and marital history of both partners."

"Is it an outpatient facility, or do they have inpatient beds?"

"They have both. Several patients who undergo treatment may need to stay overnight or even two or three nights."

"Do they have many patients?"

"More and more people are seeking help with fertility issues. Discussing about infertility or inability to conceive used to be secretive and private. Not anymore. People want to discuss the issue and find solutions instead of accepting destiny. They discuss these problems at the workplace and with their boss and want to have fertility treatment covered under their insurance as a medical problem and not as a personal sexual matter."

"Why is that there are more patients of this nature?"

"When one is thirty-five years or older, time is running out, and they want to talk about it loud to reduce their own depression and anxiety. Some of them want to have their eggs kept frozen to be used for IVF when they are more mentally prepared to have the pregnancy."

They talked to Dr. Meena again for more information about the protocols at the clinic.

"What types of doctors are specialized in this field?"

"They are gynecologists and urologists who have done more specialized training in fertility disorders. Male and female doctors work in the fertility section of the clinic. These doctors have special interest in fertility management."

"So where do they start?"

"They start with conducting a complete history and physical examination of the clients (they do not want to call them as patients) and examine both husband and wife on the initial visit. A good number of problems can be diagnosed at this level itself."

"Tell us how it is resolved at this level."

"For example, a male patient may not have testicles in the scrotum at all, or he may have erectile dysfunctions. A female patient may not have normal sexual functions due to congenital defects, or there could be anatomical problems with her reproductive organs. Some of them may have hormone deficiencies that can be treated with hormones such as follicular stimulating hormone or estrogens. They may be having thyroid disorders or pituitary disorders. Some have malnutrition and anemia or vitamin deficiencies, which are correctable."

"What is the treatment at this level?"

"Recommendation for treatment varies and depends up on the underlying causes. There are some situations where the couple just needs proper sex education. This may sound silly, but there are many societies in the Asian countries and Islamic countries where it is a taboo to talk about sexual matters. They get very little information or education in schools about reproductive matters."

"When do you recommend artificial insemination?"

"Artificial insemination is an option for certain couples. Some men may have ejaculation problems such as premature ejaculation, erectile dysfunction, low sperm count, low motility of sperms, and retrograde ejaculation. Some women may have vaginal or cervical problems but having normal tubes, ovaries, and uterus. Excessive vaginal or cervical mucous or cervical scarring can hinder the movement of sperms."

"Who is the donor of the sperms?"

"It may be possible to use the husband's sperms in certain situations. It may be necessary to obtain sperms from another donor in certain other situations. Sometimes it could be from a known per-

THE CLINIC

son, or sometimes it is from a sperm bank. If the male person has no sperms and the female is quite healthy, she may prefer to have a donor sperm baby instead of adopting a child."

"Where does genetic therapy come in the picture?"

"They also do genetic testing and genetic counseling. When necessary, they would recommend advanced gene therapy or refer them to special center in their network."

Rani and Sooraj finally went to World Fertility and Genetic Clinic in Los Angeles after making an appointment. After the initial sign-in and paperwork, a nurse interviewed them as expected. Finally, the doctor came in to talk to them. He was a pleasant, tall gentleman with European accent.

"I have already reviewed all your medical records and charts. We shall do a physical examination of both of you again for our own information, and then I shall talk to both of you."

"Okay, doctor."

After physical examination and reading various blood and urine tests, the doctor broke the result to Rani and Sooraj.

"Both of you are in good health. Rani is in good health and makes ovum regularly and has no anatomical problems in the external genitalia. Sooraj is also in good health."

"Yes, doctor."

"We want to do another sperm analysis on Sooraj. On Rani, we want to do another ultrasound and a special dye test called hysterosalpingogram."

"What is involved in this test, doctor?'

"We inject a dye into the uterus and see the flow of the dye into the fallopian tubes up to the very ends called the fimbria. This will allow us to see if the fallopian tubes are patent and functioning."

"Is it painful?"

"No. Not at all."

"What are the next steps afterward?"

"It appears from your medical records that you would be an appropriate candidate to have in-vitro fertilization. You have had two ectopic pregnancies, and the second one was life-threatening. One of your fallopian tubes has been tied off. Having said that, I would like to wait for the sperm tests and your tests to come back, and then I shall go over further details with you."

So they made appointments for those two tests the following day. Rani and Sooraj decided to stay overnight in a nearby motel. Tests went smoothly. By the afternoon, the doctor was able to sit down with them and go over the results.

"The sperm tests came back as good. Sooraj has no real problems. The sperms are motile and adequate in numbers. On Rani, we found that the right fallopian tube is completely shut off due to the last surgery. We knew that already. The left fallopian tube has one area of narrowing, which could be due to kinks or twists, since it is longer than usual. This can happen from adhesions in the pelvis."

"What does all this mean, doctor?"

"It confirms our recommendation that you are better off having in-vitro fertilization than trying for another natural pregnancy."

"If we agree for the same, what is the next step?"

"First, we need to sign certain papers, which basically provides informed consent. There are disclaimers in it, stating there will be no guarantees as to the outcome. Many things are unpredictable, and many things can go wrong. This is a package containing all the information about in-vitro fertilization and payment schedule."

"How much does it cost? Will our medical insurance cover it?"

"Your bill will be itemized. There is an initial deposit of $5,000 to get started. We do not accept the insurance, but we shall assist you to get reimbursed from your insurance company. You may or may not get reimbursed based on many issues from their point of view."

"What are the subsequent payments?"

"Payments will be required periodically as we go along the process. This may take a few months. For certain individuals, multiple attempts are needed, while some others see success on first try itself."

"What is the total bill going to be, doctor?"

"It could be anywhere from $20,000 to $100,000, depending upon variety of circumstances and number of attempts needed."

"How much time do we have to make a decision?"

"Please take your time, study everything. We can give you some reference materials to read. We can also give you names of some of the satisfied clients. It is okay with us for you to talk to them to get a better idea of their experiences. In fact, we have an annual get-together of in vitro babies and mothers for people to meet, greet, and share."

"Okay, doctor."

"I am going to give you name and contact information of one of our staff members who can talk to you more and answer any questions. She is very well versed and knowledgeable."

Rani and Sooraj came home with various documents, reference materials, and contact names. They talked to a few previous clients of World Fertility and Genetic Clinic. They also did a lot of reading and research on this topic. Some of the stories of their newly acquired friends were astounding.

Linda and Melinda were very close friends—too close in that they shared everything in their lives. They were legally married in the State of California that allows same-sex marriage. Both of them went to work during daytime and spent time together when they returned from work. They cooked and ate together, talked to each other, shared same laughs, and watched TV after dinner.

One day, Linda, the wife, told her husband, Melinda, "I want to be a mother. Rather, we need a child to raise between us."

Melinda thought about it and agreed. "Let us have a child. We can raise it between us."

They were normal adults in all aspects except for the homosexuality.

"Let us go to the World Fertility and Genetic Clinic. They will tell us how to go about it."

The doctor advised Linda that the best course of action for her was to get artificial insemination from the sperm bank.

"Do you know that you can choose the type of sperm that you like?"

They were given choices of the sperms based on race, skin color, eye color, intelligence level, and achievements. Obviously, they decided to buy the sperm of a tall Caucasian male who had college education and an IT job. They were both Caucasians. LGBTQ members have to use donor sperms to become pregnant.

In due course, Linda became pregnant. They cherished the baby girl as the best gift for their lives. Now they had objectivity for life and work.

Then they heard a story on the opposite side. They also heard the story of male homosexual couples that wanted to have a child of their own.

"How can you get pregnant?" asked one.

The other said, "We have to find a surrogate lady to carry my child for nine months. Then we can take over."

"Are you going to impregnate her by having sex with her? I cannot leave you."

"No. I don't have to have sex with her. Either she can agree for artificial insemination in the laboratory or we can do an in-vitro fertilization with an egg from the bank."

"So either way, we need to rent a uterus for nine months."

"We have been fair and equal to each other so far. If you are having a baby, then I want to have one also. We can raise them together."

The surrogate mother was arranged through the World Fertility and Genetic Clinic. They also had a happy ending.

Then there is the story of David and Susan Lindsey. They were a beautiful couple who loved each other dearly. They went to the same college and were in the same class. They were in the twenties with their entire life ahead of them. Soon after graduation from college, they decided to get married. Both of them had first-time jobs in reputable firms. Life was beautiful and looked wonderful. They were planning to have a baby after one year of honeymoon period. Fate had its way, however. They went out for dinner and a show on a Saturday night and were returning home past midnight. Destiny came in the form of a drunken driver on the wrong way, resulting in a head-on collision. Ambulance came, and they were airlifted to the nearest trauma center.

Susan miraculously escaped with minor injuries to her wrist and elbow. David, however, was comatose but had no external injuries whatsoever. Tests showed severe brain concussion and scattered areas of intracerebral bleeding. Doctors kept him on ventilator and did various treatments, including decompressing brain surgery. He remained in the intensive care unit for six months in total vegetative state. Finally, physicians gave up hope of any meaningful recovery. Family from both sides gave her maximum moral support. A decision had to be made whether to allow him to go in peace without suffering or to continue with expensive fruitless life support. At this point, Susan made an unusual request to see him live again in her womb as his child. This had never been done before. It was a strange but meaningful request.

"I want to have David's child live in me. This would be the best memorial for him, living through me."

Susan wanted to have sperms of her brain-damaged husband withdrawn surgically and artificially inseminated in her to have his child in her womb.

"We have never done this in the past. We don't even know if it will be successful or not."

"Please, doctor. This is one chance, and only once it will be possible. Please do it for David's sake."

The doctors obliged after approval by the ethics committee and after legal consultations. David's sperms stored in his seminal vesicles and prostate were withdrawn by ultrasound-guided needle puncture method and stored immediately with the sperm bank. She had the artificial insemination of her husband's sperms. Everyone was delighted when she became pregnant. David died peacefully, knowing that he was living again through Susan.

Another story is about Melissa Winslow and Rena Kaur. For different reasons both of them needed in-vitro fertilization. Rena had medical problems with diabetes mellitus, excess mucous production, and severe dyspareunia but had normal uterus and cervix, resulting in the inability to conceive naturally.

Melissa Winslow was getting depressed, moody, guilty, and panicky. Similar to many of her friends, she was focused on education and career. She was a proponent of equal rights and equal opportunities for women and was putting off marriage until she met her husband through work. He was more focused on his career and growth than her. Time was moving fast, and before she knew, she was thirty-two.

In the back of her mind, she had always wanted to be a mother and wanted to raise her own family. Now time was running out. She was unable to become pregnant by natural methods. She was not making good eggs anymore. She decided to consult the World Fertility and Genetic Clinic, having received good recommendations from one of her friends. Her biological clock was ticking.

She decided to go through the protocols of Assisted Reproductive Technology (ART). The doctors advised her that she had to make an intense effort, along with her husband. Unfortunately, her husband was not there to give her the moral or psychological support and left it all for her own to work out the details. Finally, she had also in-vitro fertilization and successful pregnancy.

World Fertility and Genetic Clinic had given Rani names of contact persons in the center who would clarify questions regarding the in-vitro fertilization. One of them was a nurse practitioner with social service background and with a lot of practical knowledge, as recommended by the doctor. Sooraj and Rani called her and had a long conversation.

"Why is this happening to women more often with so many new challenges?"

"Years ago, women got married in their twenties, did not have career ambitions, and took care of her family and home. Getting pregnant was natural and expected. Once women reach thirties, natural conception rates decline. She may not produce eggs every month, eggs may not be healthy, male partner may have less interest in sex, less number of active sperms, addictive habits start to settle in, chronic diseases crop up, and sexual dysfunction can occur. Chromosomal problems result in miscarriages. Nowadays many women are resorting to IVF (In-vitro fertilization) mostly because they are trying to get pregnant at an older age."

"Was it easy for the women in the past? I don't think so."

"Even up to one hundred years ago, in most countries, including United States, the duty of the woman was to produce children, take care of the children and the family, and do the cooking, cleaning, laundry, and other household chores. She was not expected to work or think independently. She had no voting rights, financial knowledge, or public life. Women were treated as baby conveyors and unpaid child-care providers. Producing children every year and year after year was her duty. It was considered as her duty to the state and to the family. Sex was on demand by the husband. There was no need for love or choice in matrimony. He marries her, provides shelter, security, and money. In return, she provides sex and produces children and takes care of the house. Life expectancy was low. The more children she produced, the better it is. Many may not reach adulthood. She may die from complications of childbirth. But her love to him is proven by the number of children they had."

"Are there any books by specific individuals describing their experiences?"

"Michelle Obama, former first lady, wrote in her book *Becoming* about her experiences and talked about it. After a miscarriage, she felt failed, broken, and lonely. They were trying to get pregnant, but it was not going well. She was in her thirties and felt that her biological clock was slowing and egg production was limited. So she went for IVF and took many hormone shots to beef up her reproductive efficiency. Finally, she had Malia and then Sasha born. Now they are twenty and seventeen respectively and in good health."

"Any others?"

"Other celebrities had similar problems. Actress Gabrielle Union and her husband, Dwyane Wade, had a baby with the help of a surrogate mother. Senator Tammy Duckworth, singer Beyonce, Chrissy Teigen, Khloe Kardashian are others who had miscarriages and subsequent IVF. Still, many do not talk about this topic being painful physically and emotionally, along with the stigma and ignorance and feeling of guilt and shame."

"What is the history on in-vitro fertilization?"

"Babies born by this procedure were initially called test tube babies. The first test tube baby, Louise Brown, was born forty years ago in July 1978 in the UK. Since then, over eight million babies have been born by using IVF methods."

"How common is this procedure?"

"Over 9 percent of women between the ages of thirty-five and forty-five have received various fertility treatments. Nearly 2 percent of all US births involve some type of Assisted Reproductive Technology. Twelve percent of White women, 3 percent of Black women, and 5 percent of Hispanic women are opting for the ART, the difference being mainly due to the affordability. Records show that forty-eight thousand babies were born by IVF in 2003 alone. One in five pregnancies result in miscarriage. People do not talk about their experiences because it is physically and emotionally painful. There is a stigma and ignorance also."

"How difficult is the process?"

"Women have to tune up their reproductive capacity into peak efficiency by taking hormone injections for several weeks, stay healthy, and maximize the ovulation cycles to harvest the good eggs. In the laboratory, the eggs are combined with the husband's sperms to produce the fertilized egg, which is then reintroduced inside the woman's womb. Sometimes the sperm is directly injected inside the egg to ensure fertilization. This step is called intracytoplasmic sperm injection."

"How expensive is it?"

"It costs $23,000 for a single cycle of in-vitro fertilization. Average of 2.3 to 2.7 cycles of IVF are needed for a successful result. It could take four to six weeks of time to do one cycle of attempt. The total expense from beginning to end could run into $100,000 for some."

"What is the most uncomfortable part in this process?"

"The most painful part is the procedure to harvest the eggs. Weeks of powerful hormone injections can cause many side effects and hospitalizations. Most of the cost is associated with these injections, their side effects, need for hospitalization, and finally harvesting the egg by a surgical method."

"Will the health insurance cover the expenses?"

"Insurance companies may not cover these costs as medical expenses. However, some employers are adding medical benefits to include egg freezing and miscarriages. Pregnancy-related discriminations are illegal, whether it involves loss of promotion, time off, or vacation. An employee cannot be fired because of pregnancy."

"Do you need a surrogate mother for all in-vitro fertilizations?"

THE CLINIC

"No. Sometimes it is necessary to implant the zygote or fertilized egg in a surrogate mother since the original mother is unable to carry on with the pregnancy. Certain people may have had a hysterectomy done for benign disease but had the ovaries left in place that are functioning and still producing eggs. So she can have her eggs fertilized with her healthy husband's sperms outside the body, and then the zygote is implanted inside another woman. This person is called a surrogate mother. In other words, her womb is being rented for the purpose of holding the fetus to full term."

"Who will arrange for the surrogate, if one is needed?"

"The World Fertility and Genetic Clinic arranges all the protocols, find the surrogate mother, execute all the documents and contracts, and carry out the in-vitro fertilization."

"Does premarital evaluation need checkup with the fertility clinic?"

"Modern-day couples want premarital consultations and genetic tests done through the World Fertility and Genetic Clinic or similar facilities. They want to know the risk of developing diseases and health-care risk for the person they are going to marry. They want to know of any genetic or congenital disorders that can be passed on to their children before getting married. They want to have cancer screening and blood tests on each other to diagnose current and future illnesses. After the baby is conceived, they want to study the genetic makeup of the fetus in utero. Similar to prenuptial agreement for financial matters, premarital screening for genetic disorders, degenerative disorders, risk for cancers and other familial illnesses is a good step."

"We heard Chinese people are getting into fertility clinics in larger numbers?"

"Chinese people are coming to the USA in large numbers to seek help from the fertility clinics in the USA because the Chinese government has relaxed the rule on one child per family. They are now allowed to have more children, and the Chinese women are in a hurry to get babies. They can opt for in vitro or in vivo fertilizations. Chinese scientists and fertility clinics are hacking the US clinics to obtain genetic technology. Chinese mining companies own several fertility clinics covertly to make money on them and to steal technology. This has become one of the sticking points between the US and China in their trade negotiations."

"Any unusual news on this topic?"

"A newspaper article reported that after twenty-seven years of deep-freezing, an embryo was used again successfully for creating a child. Molly Everette Gibson was born this way from an embryo that was frozen in 1992. It was thawed and transferred to the uterus of Tina Gibson. These are leftover embryos from couples that had pursued in-vitro fertilization. Usually these unwanted embryos are discarded. The National Embryo Donation Center can deep-freeze them and give them to those who prefer to have them as a way of having a child instead of adopting a full-born child."

"How big is this issue of fertility concerns?"

"Roughly seventy-eight thousand children born in 2017 [1.7 percent of all newborns a year] were conceived with the help of assisted reproduction technology. Embryo adoption is only 5 percent of them. This provides another option between in-vitro fertilization and adoption of babies. The mother can experience the pregnancy as if a surrogate mother."

"What are the legalities that have been noted?"

"In the future, obstetrics and gynecology doctors must detect and correct congenital anomalies in utero, failing which the doctors will be held liable for malpractice. A fetus was diagnosed to have Down syndrome. Mother wanted the child aborted. State of Ohio law makes it a felony as infanticide by mother and the genetic counselor and physician charged as coconspirators. December 17, 2017, Ohio law says it is a criminal offense to abort a child because of genetic conditions. One option is to treat and rectify these genetic disorders inside the uterus before the baby is born by using advanced gene technology. World Genetic Research Laboratory is equipped for this type of work."

Rani said, "Thank you so much for talking to us. You were a great help."

She answered, "Please take your time and feel free to call anytime if you have any further questions."

Chapter 3

The Process

Rani called the World Fertility and Genetic Clinic after two months. She wanted to go ahead with in-vitro fertilization. She made an appointment to start definitive measures. She had filled out the consent forms signed by herself and Sooraj. She also made the initial deposit of $5,000.

They went to see the doctor the following week as per appointment.

He said, "We have all your records, and you have already completed all necessary tests. The paperwork has been completed, and the accounting department has given us the okay to proceed further."

"So what is the next step?"

"We can break this down into five general steps—one, ovary stimulation. Two, egg retrieval. Three, insemination. Four, fertilization and embryo culture. And five, embryo transfer."

"First, I am going to give you a special hormone injection. It is called human gonadotropic hormone or HCG. It will stimulate your ovary to make good eggs in larger quantity. Only then we can harvest your eggs. For certain individuals, we may have to give additional hormones such as follicular stimulating hormone (FSH) and luteinizing hormone (LH)."

"How long will this take to be effective?"

"These are taken over eight to fourteen days. At that point, we shall do an ultrasound and blood tests to know if the ovaries are ripe enough for egg retrieval."

"Are there any complications or side effects for these hormones?"

"Yes. Some people feel heartburn, nausea, vomiting, loss of appetite, weight gain, and abdominal pain or cramps. The swollen ovaries can cause these symptoms, and when in excess, it is called ovarian hyperstimulation syndrome (OHSS). Sometimes they may even need admission to the hospital for treatment."

"What happens afterward?"

"During the second stage, we perform the egg retrieval if the ovaries are ripe and ready. This will require a minor procedure in the operating room under heavy sedation."

"How is this done?"

"The first choice is to do a procedure called transvaginal ultrasound-guided needle aspiration. A thin needle is advanced through the sidewall of the vagina to puncture the ovarian follicle and suction out the eggs. Ultrasound is used to guide the needle to correct location. Several eggs will be retrieved during one trial and immediately placed in the culture medium."

"Are there any complications, doctor?"

"Yes. Things can go wrong. One can cause bleeding, infection, puncture of bladder or bowel. Some patients complain of pelvic pain."

"Is it always successful?"

"Not always. For some patients, this technique is not easy. Then we have to do the egg retrieval by laparoscopic method. In that case, we have to give a regular anesthesia, make a small cut near the umbilicus, and pass a lighted scope into the abdominal cavity. Thus, we can do it under direct vision."

"I assume it is a bigger operation with more risks?"

"Yes and no. You need stronger anesthesia and small cut. But the procedure is done under better control."

"What is the next stage?"

"This next part is done in the laboratory. We place the eggs in the IVF culture medium. In the meantime, your husband would provide sperms, which are also placed in the culture medium. Then we select the best eggs and best sperms to come together and place them in the incubator. The sperms enter into the eggs, and fertilization takes place."

"Then what happens?"

"Now we wait to see the result, which may take two to four days. The actual fertilization may take only one or two hours. By next day, we can see two nuclei, and by the second day, we can see four cells on the embryo. By the third day, it may have six to ten cells."

"When do you transfer into my uterus?"

"It will be ready in about three days."

"Does that also need a surgery?"

"No. It can be done under sedation. No surgery is involved. The fertilized embryo is suspended in a drop of fluid, drawn inside a long thin tube with a syringe at the end. This tube is gently threaded inside the uterus and deposited inside the uterus."

"Then what happens?"

"You need to be in complete bed rest for two or three hours and in partial rest for the next two days. We may do a rehearsal or a mock embryo transfer while we are waiting for the embryo to mature the day before the actual transfer. This way, we would know about your anatomy, tolerance, and technology. We will also give you progesterone hormone ahead of time to make the uterus more receptive."

"When do I know it is successful and has gotten implanted in the uterus?"

"We have to give it a few days. We can do pregnancy hormone level checks and ultrasound examination. If it is stable in four weeks, then we can relax."

"What can go wrong?"

"Sometimes it does not get attached to the uterus. Sometimes it can become an ectopic again."

"What do we do if it does not attach inside the uterus and washes off?"

"The good part is that we always have several embryos that would have hatched in the culture medium. We freeze them and store them. We can try another one of them for implantation again after a few days."

"If the first time is successful, what do you do with those other frozen embryos?"

"We generally keep them for a while, and sometimes we donate them to others who cannot make their own embryos. Certain women prefer accepting an embryo as a better choice than adopting a child."

Having satisfied themselves with all the questions, their own conversation with others, and their own reading, Rani was mentally and physically ready. She signed in and underwent the shots and tolerated the discomfort with pleasure. She went for the egg retrieval, and Sooraj donated the sperms on the same day. It was painful for Rani, and she had to stay at the hospital overnight. Two days later, she had a rehearsal implant, and the following day, she had the real embryo transfer. She was happy to go through the tests and procedures no matter how uncomfortable they were. The goal was to become a mother whatever it takes.

After two more days of rest, she came home. One week later, she tested herself on urine stick.

"Yes, it is positive! She cried loud."

Three weeks later, she went for checkup at the center. Blood tests were positive, and ultrasound showed the tiny baby inside the uterus.

It was the day of celebration for Rani and Sooraj. "Yes, we did it."

They were full of smiles and satisfaction. But they would not disclose it to anyone for a few more weeks, including their parents, just to be safe.

Chapter 4

The Surrogate

Rani and Sooraj met several people and made many good friends who were in the same predicament as she was during the last one and a half years. They even joined a meetup group to discuss common concerns. It was comforting to hear other people's problems and compare with hers. It was during one of those evenings when she heard about surrogate mothers to have a child of yours, but you are unable to carry the pregnancy yourself due to various medical problems. Karen told her an expansive story on this.

Karen Dran and her husband, Vincent Dran, had done extensive research online and had numerous personal discussions with friends and physicians. She was only thirty-one years old, and Vincent was thirty-six. They had been married for five years now, and they very much wanted to have their own child.

"What was wrong and why could you not conceive?"

"Unfortunately, I had a miscarriage one year after I got married. Then the same thing happened next year also. Then I started to get excessive bleeding during periods."

"Then what happened?"

"I ended up going to the gynecologist for more consultations. They wanted to do an endometrial biopsy."

"And?"

"That is when they told me that I had a uterine disease that is premalignant. The biopsies showed I had a condition called atypical endometrial hyperplasia with several abnormal-looking cells. Left alone, I would develop cancer of the uterus soon."

"What about pregnancy?"

"The doctor said I would not hold the pregnant baby and will continue to have miscarriages. But the worse news was that the doctors advised me to have a hysterectomy, leaving the ovaries in place as the best course of action."

"That is terrible news."

"It was heartbreaking for a young couple like us. But the decision had to be made. Cancer of the uterus is worse scenario."

"So you had a hysterectomy?"

"Yes. Now it is three years after the hysterectomy, and I am otherwise in good health. The desire to have our baby is stronger than ever. I want my own child one way or another."

"Did you think about adopting a child?"

"Yes. We tossed around the idea of adopting a child. It was too expensive and a long drawn-out process. Also, we wanted our own child instead of raising someone else's child."

"So you went for surrogate pregnancy?"

"Yes. We decided to have our baby with a surrogate mother as a better choice. It will be our genes and chromosomes but just incubating it in a rented womb for nine months. We have both healthy eggs and sperms. Why not use them when they are available?"

"So how did you find this place in India?"

"We started a website search and then talked to some friends. It was a long process indeed. We wanted to find the best place to have a surrogate pregnancy. We embarked on another long search. The best location and facility we found was around the globe in India!"

"What is the name of this facility?"

"It is called ART Hospital. ART Hospital is a gleaming nine-story building in a large campus with a walking garden located in the outskirts of Mumbai. ART stands for Assisted Reproductive Technology."

"What is so special about it?"

"It is a one-stop hospital that will provide the entire spectrum of needs and requirements of clients in this field. They have a full-

THE CLINIC

fledged maternity hospital with operating theater and staff. They have all amenities to do egg harvesting, laparoscopic procedures, anesthesia, sperm banking, and genetic laboratory to conduct in-vitro fertilization."

"Do they arrange the surrogates?"

"But most important of all is that they have a steady supply of surrogate mothers from rural India who will do the job of carrying the pregnancy for money, far cheaper than anywhere else in the world."

"It looks like medical tourism. Did you check out the reviews?"

"The reviews online were excellent. Many Europeans, Australians, and Americans have had successful outcome here. Testimonials from celebrities and movie stars and politicians are abounding. Pictures of newborns and happy mothers of different ethnicity were displayed."

"What about the staff and doctors?"

"Staffing review showed well-qualified and well-trained physicians, nurses, and technicians."

"How are their results?"

"The reports indicated they were doing average one or two surrogate deliveries every week. They were claiming over 70 percent success in implanting the zygote on the first attempt. Statistics indicated the medical tourism in the field of assisted reproduction and fertility was the major activity in this small suburban town."

They had a Zoom interview with the director of the institution. Her name is Anita Kulkarni, and she was a specialist in fertility matters trained in India and in the US. She put them at ease with a pleasant demeanor and encouraged them to go there and spend a few days at the campus.

"We have a special guest quarters with all Western amenities. It is an air-conditioned two-bedroom cottage with kitchen and a maidservant. You may spend a few days there, go through the facilities, talk to people, and make yourself comfortable."

"Is there a cost involved for the accommodation and food?"

"The charges are fair market rate as any other four-star hotel room. Food can be taken from the hospital cafeteria, or it can be freshly cooked at your cottage with the help of the maid assigned to the unit. The average cost of accommodation and food will total about $200 per day. If you are planning to undergo any procedures during the visit, then the charges will be further subsidized to bare minimum."

"How about if we stay at a facility away from the hospital and just come over to visit?"

"No problem. There are some modest hotels in the neighborhood where the Indian patients and clients stay due to cost considerations. However, the on-campus guesthouses are preferred by foreigners because of many convenience factors."

"Is there a liaison or representative who can spend more time with us when we get there?'

"Yes. We have an excellent English-speaking liaison for European and American clients. Her name is Manisha Roy. I shall forward her contact information to your email address. She will totally coordinate all your care, your visit, stay, and treatment and walk you through every step of the way. We encourage you to come over as a medical tourist. We assure you the best results. You will be happy with your newborn baby. It will be your genes, your child. We guarantee full satisfaction. I shall have Manisha take over your case, and she will be contacting you soon."

True enough, Manisha contacted the Drans the next day by phone as well as by email, offering her services to help them in any way. After a couple of missed calls and timing issues, they made the connection. Karen and Vincent had a few more questions to her about the process.

"So tell us how this works, how long it takes and what are the protocols."

Manisha was happy to go over the steps.

"First thing is for you to feel comfortable with us and be confident that you will be proud parents of your own child. Basically, we are using your own egg and your own sperm to fertilize the zygote. Then this zygote is implanted inside the uterus of a surrogate woman. She carries the pregnancy to full term for you on your behalf. When the baby is delivered, you take possession of your child and go home and be happy."

"It sounds simple. What are the legalities?"

"We arrange all documents and complete all formalities, anything and everything on your behalf."

"How do you arrange the surrogate?"

"We have a big group of good surrogates in our wait list. We prescreen the surrogate woman to make sure that she is in good health, she is under no force or pressure, and are totally willing to cooperate in the entire process."

"Do we get to select one lady among a short list three or five candidates?"

"No problem. You are looking for a lineup? Please remember that these are working ladies who have to take the day off and travel a distance to come here. They have to be compensated for the day and travel."

"Do we get to talk to the attorney?"

"Yes. We have an attorney who is always on board to answer any legal questions and to have properly executed contracts by the surrogates and the prospective parents so that everyone is protected."

"How do we know that the surrogate lady is going to comply with all the precautions for a good pregnancy?"

"We keep them on campus and take care of them for the entire duration of the pregnancy."

"How do you do that?"

"We have fifty rooms in the basement of the building which are dedicated to accommodate the surrogates. They are expected to stay in the campus and follow instructions. They are given good nourishing food, vitamins, and prenatal care. They are residing on campus all the time to address any emergencies."

"How well are they taken care of?"

"They have common areas, bathrooms, cafeteria, and recreation down there. They are taken out for exercise outdoors daily. They are tested periodically with blood tests and urine tests. They are given regular medical checkups. All such good care is free."

"How are they paid?"

"They are paid well for their service. Entire salary can be saved for future use, since there is no out-of-pocket expense for them for one whole year."

"Out of curiosity, how much money are they paid?"

"You don't have to worry about that part. We take care of it. It is included in the package fee we are charging you. By local standards, they get one hundred times more money than they would be making by any type of daily labor. Moreover, they are living free for nearly a year with excellent care."

"When do we give our egg and sperms? How long should we stay at your place?"

"During your first visit, after you have inspected our facility and talked to our staff and if you are comfortable, then you can sign the appropriate consent forms and documents. Harvesting the egg from Karen may require a few days and some preliminary treatments and tests. She may have to undergo a small procedure under anesthesia. Collecting the sperms will be much easier."

"What happens next?"

"The eggs and sperms are deep frozen until the surrogate is prepared for receiving the zygote. Once everything is ready, then the egg and sperm are thawed and fertilized. The living fertilized zygote is then implanted inside the uterus of the surrogate."

"How long further it will take to know that the baby is growing?"

"It will take a few days to ensure that the zygote has safely implanted itself. Give or take one-month time should be adequate for everything if we move along without wasting any time."

"You mean we can leave after one month?"

"Yes, if everything goes well. There could be roadblocks on the way. It may need more time for harvesting good eggs."

"What happens after we leave? How do we know she is doing the right things to carry on with the pregnancy?"

"We take care of it for you. We can communicate with you and the surrogate regularly over digital platforms such as FaceTime or Zoom."

"When do we come back for second visit?"

THE CLINIC

"You can come back when it is time for delivery, when the baby is full term. That will be about nine months later."

"Will there be a long wait for the delivery at that time?"

"We can arrange a C-section for safe delivery of the baby on the predetermined day so that you can take charge of the baby without much waiting."

"Will it not be an unnecessary C-section, being done for convenience, ignoring the mother's health?"

"For us and you, the baby is more important. I am sure that you will be of the same opinion also. Your baby's health (or life) is more precious than that of the hired help. I am sorry to put it bluntly like that."

Karen and Vincent were speechless for a while.

"Is it possible for us to ship our egg and sperm from USA in deep frozen package? This way we can come to your location at the end of nine months to take charge of the baby, thus avoiding the first visit?"

"Yes, it can be done. We are affiliated with World Fertility and Genetic Clinic. We are part of a worldwide franchise network. However, it will be more reassuring for some individuals to be here in person at the beginning and at the end of the process."

Finally, Karen and Vincent made arrangements for a trip to India after making a definitive appointment with ART Hospital. Manisha had made all necessary arrangements to receive them from Mumbai airport and bring them to the hospital. They were impressed with the efficiency and arrangements for their stay. They could get a car with driver for $30 a day. They could have custom-made home-cooked meals prepared by the maidservant for $10 a day. They could take a short walk for a half mile to reach the beach or go to town for shopping or eating. People were courteous and helpful.

They decided to stay for a month, donate their egg and sperm, and watch their zygote being implanted in the surrogate lady. Total bill for the entire one-month stay and surrogate pregnancy was $30,000. It will not be covered by the medical insurance. Everything went well as per plans.

"Did you like the surrogate lady?"

"Yes. She was a nice lady. She appeared to be in good health and was interested in doing this for us. She saw it as a service to us more than as a profit-making venture. She had three children of her own with her husband."

"Was she comfortable and at ease with all the regulations?"

"We are not sure, but she was willing to go through with it. It appeared that she was missing her family for almost one year, since she is mandated to stay at the campus."

"Have you heard of instances where major disagreement broke out between the surrogate mother and biological parents?"

"Yes, it is reported. In a certain instance, the surrogate felt too attached to the baby, being her own firstborn also, and refused to give up the baby."

"Any other stories?"

"In one instance, the gene test during the pregnancy indicated that the baby may have chromosomal anomalies and the baby may be mentally deficient. So the biological parents wanted to abort the baby and start over, but the surrogate refused abortion. She said she would raise the child the way it is born. Her motherhood feelings and religious beliefs were quite strong."

"So when did you go back to India to get the child?"

"As suggested, we were tracking the progress on FaceTime and Zoom. We returned nine months later to see our baby being delivered by Cesarean section."

"Did you stay at the same cottage at the hospital?"

"Yes. It was all prearranged as before. We must say they were very efficient and reliable."

"You must be happy now."

"Yes. We were ecstatic and thrilled to have our own baby, legally ours."

"Did the surrogate lady give you any trouble such as not wanting to give up the child or some other stunt?"

"Actually, she was happy to give away the child, since she had her own children to deal with."

"How was it to hold your son in your own hands?"

"It was an exhilarating experience. I had goose bumps. I loved it."

"What was the next plan?"

"We had to arrange for the return trip to the USA."

"There must have been some help on this from the ART Hospital."

"Yes. They provided us with necessary documents about the surrogate-delivered child, DNA verifications, and certificates with photographs. We took them to the US consulate in Mumbai."

"Did they give you any trouble?"

"Not really, but they needed a few days to complete their own verifications and immigration documents."

"What was their main concern?"

"The US consulate wanted to ensure that this is not an adopted baby but our own. DNA analysis and verification between parents and child was part of the documentation. Sworn testimony by the parents was also recorded."

"The hospital must have had prior track record on these protocols."

"Yes, ART Hospital was familiar with these protocols. They had several foreign parents coming to India for surrogate childbirth. Their help was valuable."

"How was the return journey?"

"No problems to talk about. We reached safely back home."

"How is the baby now?"

"He is named David and is fourteen pounds now. He is happy and healthy. Here is his picture."

Chapter 5

The Bank

Sooraj had a lot of free time to walk around, explore, and talk to various people at the World Fertility and Genetic Clinic while Rani was undergoing tests and hormone treatments and getting prepared for the in-vitro fertilization. He used the time to go around, look over various amenities and different sections. He engaged in conversations with different employees.

One section that he was forced to visit was the sperm bank, where he was to donate his sperms on the same day as egg retrieval for Rani. He talked to the technician there and gathered a lot of information as to how the sperm bank works. They chatted for a long time. He told Sooraj about the university students who come there to donate sperms for money. He told him about the story of John Edwards.

John Edwards was a very bright student. He graduated from the high school as the valedictorian of his class. But he came from a broken family and had never met his father. His mother raised him single-handedly, and he went through a lot of hardship in his childhood. He worked in various odd jobs to support himself through the school days. It was with the mentorship of his science teacher that he was able to keep himself focused on the academics. He grew up as a tall, handsome young man with blue eyes and blond hair. He was accepted to college with scholarship at Yale and Harvard. He joined Yale, being closer to his hometown in Connecticut. Still, he had to come up with money every month to meet his personal expenses

THE CLINIC

and food and stay. The scholarship covered only the tuition. He had taken a student loan but still had to make up the difference by working on odd jobs.

That was when he met a certain recruiter through his friend in the dorm. The recruiter was a middle-aged man with a big smile and a potbelly. He had many friends and acquaintances in the college over the years and was a frequent visitor to the campus.

"I have an easy option for you to make an extra $500 a month," he told John.

That was how he learned about the sperm bank in the neighborhood. All he had to do was to donate his semen to the sperm bank once a month.

So he made an appointment with them to know more about it.

The sperm bank had interviewed him, made a profile, and took a photograph. They told him that most other donors were getting only $100 per deposit. However, they considered his profile excellent, so they offered him $500 for each deposit.

Sooraj learned more about the functioning of the sperm bank very quickly.

Sperm banking is a $4 billion industry according to 2018 statistics. It is estimated that thirty thousand to sixty thousand children are born each year in the USA through the help of sperm banks. About 20 percent of the clients are heterosexual couple, 60 percent of them are gay women, and the remaining 20 percent are single moms by choice.

"Why are the sperm banks located close to universities?" he wondered.

"Because the donors are likely to be intelligent students. They get paid a decent amount of dollars for the donation. Fraternity organizations are used as recruiting facilities. They are young, often athletic, and educated."

"How much do the recipients have to pay to get the sperms?"

"Price for the client getting the sperms is anywhere from $1,100 to $5,000 for one vial and will need at least five vials for one successful pregnancy. If a woman wants two children from the same father, the price could go over $10,000."

Some donors are in high demand because of their features such as White race, blue eyes, and dark hair with tall and athletic look. Sperm banks offer information such as bio data, educational status, and physical descriptions about the donor and also a photograph, if needed.

"How is it in other countries?"

"In the international scene, Denmark sperm donors have the highest reputation. They are of good height, good skin color, eye color, good education, and blond hair. They are in demand in over fifty countries."

"Can they bring it over to the USA?"

"FDA has banned import of sperms from any other country due to fear of communicable diseases that started with mad cow disease."

"How has this Covid-19 affected college life?"

"Due to the covid-19 pandemic, sperm banks were running low in their supplies, since the donors are hesitant to go to the banks. There was too much demand to have a pandemic baby, and desperate women are turning into unregulated Facebook groups to find donors. Sperm kings are getting exhausted. Kyle Gordy of Malibu, California, has already fathered thirty-five children, and five more are on the way."

"Are there support groups for this?"

"One such Facebook group is Sperm Donation USA, which is an eleven-thousand-member private group."

"What other media groups are available?"

"There are apps and websites to bypass the official banks. Apps for finding a donor are Modamily, Just a Baby, and KnownDonorRegistry. Natal donor is for instructions on sperm shipping tools. Dadikit is for sperm analysis and storage. Some donors and clients are making direct contact and meet in Airbnb arrangements for short periods."

"What are the steps in making the donation?"

"The donors have to undergo registration, questions, blood tests, and verification of illnesses and genetic disorders, each time before donation. The collected sperm has to be quarantined for six months."

THE CLINIC

Yet another fact that he did not know was that the fertility clinic was affiliated with several other such clinics across the country as a franchise. They also had branches and offices in many different countries. All of them were interconnected through a secretive website called DWS, which stood for Deep Whale Surfing or Dark Web Site. All of them were also interacting with a large genetic laboratory functioning in an unknown location. This genetic laboratory conducts very advanced research and treatments unavailable anywhere else in the world.

Another function of the World Fertility and Genetic Clinic is to help women to freeze their ovum for future use. Some of them are very focused and successful career women.

One such person was Melissa, who was thirty-four years old and was planning to marry her boyfriend soon. But suddenly he broke up with her when the COVID-19 pandemic started, and she was left alone. Because of the pandemic, lockdown, and isolation precautions, she could not even think of meeting new dates. Her life was getting complicated, and her pathway to motherhood was delayed, and time was running out. It will take at least three or four years to meet someone and become close enough to marry and raise a family. That was when she decided to get a consultation with the World Fertility and Genetic Clinic to freeze her ova for future use, as suggested by one of her close friends. She could fertilize it in vitro with a chosen man's sperm and have it implanted back in her own uterus, even if she gets to forty years of age.

Many single women have been freezing their monthly ovum for reuse three and four years later.

"How much does it cost to freeze the eggs?"

"The cost of one egg freezing can be $6,500 to $18,000, and insurance companies will not cover that."

"Why do women freeze their eggs?"

"For a single woman in her thirties with no steady dates and full-fledged career in mind, egg freezing is better than adoption. After some time, loneliness sets in, and the desire to have one's own family and children becomes overwhelming. The frozen egg comes in handy."

Sooraj engaged in a conversation with a technician who demanded confidentiality.

"The sperm bank collects and preserves male sperms donated on a voluntary basis. At times, it is collected involuntarily also without the knowledge of the donor. Yes, it is illegal, but it is for special reasons. These are high-value men who are targeted by certain specially trained ladies working for the bank. The bank uses it for artificial insemination of one or more women."

"So who are the people getting help from the sperm bank?"

"Sometimes it is used for a man's own sexual partner who is unable to conceive due to anatomical problems in her vagina or cervix but otherwise able to produce the ovum. Here the collected sperm is inserted into the uterus with help of a physician."

"What other types of women want to get artificial insemination besides those whose who have medical problems?"

"More often it is used by women who want to become mother of a child without commitment to a male partner. It could be a lesbian or a single career woman who does not want a male partner in her life. Heterosexual couples with male infertility have option of adopting a child or seeking help of a sperm bank."

"Does the woman know as to whose sperm she is using to get pregnant?"

"Yes and no. Very often it is kept anonymous. However, the sperm bank keeps all the records for future verification. Sometimes she is choosing the type of baby she wants based on height, weight, education, skin color, and race of the donor. Also, a donor can make a direct donation to a specific individual and can agree to provide identifying information to the mother and offspring."

"What are some other choices?"

"Sometimes the woman is using her own husband's sperm. Sometimes she wants to choose the best progeny that she desires. Norwegian males are tall and handsome. She can choose one with college degree or athletic ability or a high achiever."

"Can the donor claim biological fatherhood afterward? On the reverse, can he be held liable for child support?"

THE CLINIC

"When a donor gives a sperm donation, it is generally understood that he gives up all rights to the newborn and he cannot claim fatherhood. This is called third-party reproduction. The same applies to the mother and child—they cannot claim fatherhood or child support from the donor. The fact remains that he is still the biological father.

Some children want to find out their biological father out of curiosity even though the donor is not intending to be the legal father. In Germany, a child fifteen years or older is legally allowed to find out details about the biological father from the sperm bank."

"Are there state or local rules that govern the functioning of sperm banks?"

"Sperm banks are subject to state and local regulations, but such regulations vary widely between states and countries. Generally the donor anonymity is enforced, and the sperm donation is limited to a small number of recipients."

"Does the woman who got pregnant from the sperm bank have to report the result to them?"

"Yes. The woman who had successful pregnancy is expected to report the result to the sperm bank for accurate record-keeping, including the donor information."

"How do they ensure the sperm is healthy and will not transmit any diseases?"

"The sperm bank is expected to verify the health of the donor for any genetic disorders and communicable diseases. He is also checked for any other illnesses. These and the quality and motility of the sperms are reverified before the final donation is done after a waiting period of six months. A lawsuit was filed in 2017 in Illinois for a child born with autism. The donor was known to have had ADHD, and the sperm bank did not reject him."

"What are some chances for abuse?"

"One GYN physician impregnated over three hundred women using his own sperm without knowledge or permission from the women. The Dark Web Site sells the sperms that are collected from high-value donors such as top scientists, politicians, CEOs of Fortune 500 companies or powerful dictators to the highest bidder.

There are some women who want the chosen one to be the father of their child."

"Do the sperm donors get paid?"

"Payment to the donor is usually around $100 per donation. It can go up to $500 in certain university communities. Recipients pay much higher fees to cover the cost of the clinic and procedure and could run into several thousand dollars. High-value donors such as those with high level of education, race, and reputation can demand higher fee."

"What are the steps involved in making a sperm donation?"

"There are many protocols involved in making a donation, and they are enforced. First, the donor signs a contract with the sperm bank, which lasts for six to twenty-four months. A specific date and time are set for the donation. The man is to avoid sex or masturbation for three days prior to this date. A complete history and physical examination is done prior to this. The donation must take place at the premises of the sperm bank to ensure validity of the donor. The donor ejaculates into a special collection condom or to a container."

"So what does the sperm bank do after the collection?"

"The ejaculate is immediately mixed with chemicals to extend the collection and to store it in multiple containers for multiple uses. The first visit donation is used to verify the quality of the sperms, motility, and quantity and discarded. Only subsequent visit donations are accepted if they pass the test during the first visit. The collected material is frozen and quarantined for six months, at which time the donor is again retested for any diseases or disorders. Only then the sperm is thawed and released for use."

"Is the donation always anonymous?"

"Usually yes. Both donor and recipient do not know the outcome of the donation. Donor does not know who gets it, and recipient does not know the source. However, a donor can make a direct donation to a specific individual and can agree to provide identifying information to the mother and offspring if both parties agree."

"What is the history on this procedure and how did it all start?"

"In 1884, Professor William Pancoast of Jefferson Medical College in Philadelphia is credited with first artificial insemination.

THE CLINIC

A married couple had visited him for infertility. The husband was found to be infertile. The lady was given anesthetic, and the professor asked one of his students to donate fresh sperms by masturbation. The student selected was by consensus vote. The material collected was taken in a syringe and was then inseminated high up into the vagina of the woman. At the request of the husband, the entire matter was kept secret. The woman became pregnant, thinking it was by natural means by her husband. Addison David Hard revealed the case in 1909 when it was written up in *American Journal of Medical World*."

"Have there been lawsuits related to artificial insemination?"

"In 1954, the Superior Court of Cook County, Illinois, granted a husband permission to divorce his wife on the grounds that she had artificial insemination without his permission. The child was considered born out of wedlock and, thus, illegitimate. In 1973, the Uniform State Law and American Bar Association approved uniform parentage act. If the wife had artificial insemination done under supervision of a qualified physician and with consent of the husband, then the child is considered legitimate, and both parents have legal rights over the child, and the husband is considered the legal father."

Chapter 6

The Gene Test

Rani was making good progress with her pregnancy. She had called her parents and also her in-laws and conveyed the good news. Everyone was jubilant and happy. They talked on FaceTime and on Zoom. They wished they could see her in person. Sooraj was helping her with groceries and other household chores, making her rest as much as possible. This was a precious baby.

All of a sudden, twelve weeks into the pregnancy, Rani got a call from World Fertility and Genetic Clinic. They wanted her to have a gene test done.

Her first reaction was, "Why? We never heard of gene testing for other people."

The clinic said she was welcome to talk it over with her gynecologist, Dr. Meena, who would be most likely providing necessary prenatal care and attend to her delivery as a neighborhood doctor.

Rani made an appointment with Dr. Meena for a prenatal checkup and to ask questions about gene testing. Rani was progressing normally with her pregnancy. The ultrasound showed normal expected development of the fetus. Rani's weight and blood tests were also normal.

"Doctor, why do they want a gene testing now?"

Dr. Meena answered, "This is a protocol nowadays. If the child is born with any birth defects or congenital disorders, the doctors are blamed for not detecting it early on."

"What are some such disorders?"

THE CLINIC

"Chromosomal abnormalities, such as Down syndrome, Turner's syndrome, Klinefelter syndrome or blood disorders like sickle cell disease, thalassemia or other conditions such as cystic fibrosis, Tay Sachs disease, retinal dystrophy are some examples."

"What can they do if some abnormality is detected?"

"Attempts can be made to correct some of these conditions by doing gene therapy while the baby is still in the mother's womb. Certain individuals would want to have it aborted and start new."

"Neither of us have any familial disorders. Is there any other reason to do the gene testing?"

"Yes. They also do this for patients having in-vitro fertilization to ensure the DNA of the baby matches the DNA of parents. Occasionally errors can happen in the laboratory where a mix-up occurs. It is not common but can happen. You could be carrying someone else's baby because of the mix-up."

"You are not kidding."

"No, I am not. I knew of a true story that ended up in a big lawsuit. A White American couple, Caucasian origin, had IVF. The child that came out was a Black African origin. The lab admitted fault resulting from a mix-up of specimens."

"Oh God, how can they let it happen?"

"No one wants to make a mistake on purpose. In spite of all the precautions, still mistakes happen. That is part of life."

"So how do they do this test?"

"First, they would simply draw a little bit of your blood."

"How does that test the baby's problems?"

"A small amount of the baby's genes is floating in the mother's blood through the placenta."

"What kinds of gene tests are done?"

"They can be one of three—one is on the genes, by testing the molecules in the DNA, sequences of the chemicals, and the individual nucleotides. Second is the whole chromosome or long segments of DNA. Finally, it is also on the proteins associated with them."

"How much does it cost?"

"Anywhere from $100 to $2,000."

"Will my insurance cover it?"

"Generally yes, if it is ordered as prenatal care by me."

"Is this blood test adequate?"

"Sometimes they will have to do more testing. This will be in the form of testing some fluid inside your uterus. This fluid is called the amniotic fluid. The baby is floating in this fluid as it is growing inside your body."

"How is that test done?"

"They would use a fine needle to draw out some of the fluid, generally done with an ultrasound guidance."

"Will that be definitive?"

"Sometimes they may need to get a sample from the placenta or from the umbilical cord of the baby. But they are very rare and only for advanced care."

"I want to think it over and talk to my husband also."

"Sure, take your time."

It was time for Rani and Sooraj to do more reading, searches, and consultation with friends. She also wanted to talk it over with her friends and compare notes with new acquaintances through the Lamaze classes she had started attending.

They learned a lot of new information about gene testing. It is now routine to do mother's blood testing in what is called NIPT, which stands for Noninvasive Prenatal Testing, which looks for floating cell-free DNA, also called cfDNA. These are particles that come from placenta, which is identical to DNA of the fetus. (This is opposed to ctDNA, which detects circulating tumor DNA to detect cancers and their follow-up in therapy.)

If there was any question or if further clarification were needed, they would do whole chromosomal study to detect conditions such as Down syndrome, which is trisomy 21 where there are three chromosomes on the twenty-first chromosome instead of two. There can be other trisomy or monosomy, all of which can lead to various congenital disorders.

Newborn children are also routinely screened for common thirty-five genetic conditions. These are tests on proteins and enzymes only.

Gene testing could be done on a single gene for a specific disorder or panel screening for groups of diseases or large-scale genomic testing for complex medical histories or for research purpose. Nearly seventy thousand different gene tests are in current use, and many more are being developed.

"There must be a lot of money in this technology," wondered Sooraj.

"Years ago, genes and gene sequencing were patentable. However, Supreme Court ruled against it, and the US government also banned it. This has allowed the technology to be shared by many laboratories all over the world and has helped to advance medical science. So there is not that much money in it, but there is business profit."

"Has gene testing helped the society in general?"

"Yes. Development of vaccine for COVID-19 infection in a short time using mRNA technology was an example of how genetic modifications have helped mankind."

"What happens when the gene test comes back as abnormal?"

"It is not uncommon for people to feel angry, depressed, guilty, and anxious and go through emotional, social, and financial crisis when a gene test comes back as abnormal. However, it also allows the parents to take early actions to treat or correct such disorders."

Rani took the blood test through Dr. Meen's office, which was analyzed for the routine screening. She was holding her fingers crossed. They both prayed for good luck and waited for the results to come back.

Chapter 7

The Laboratory

By God's grace, Rani's tests came back as good, identifying correct DNA between the baby and the parents and no gross abnormalities. There was no need for amniocentesis. It was another big relief and a day of celebration for Rani and Sooraj. They called their parents on Zoom and conveyed the good news.

Rani turned out to be lucky with the genetic test done at the twelfth week of pregnancy. However, two other couples in her Lamaze class were not so lucky. The rest of the nine couples in her class were also fine with their tests. Everyone felt sorry for these two who had problems and gathered around them for more information and for expression of sympathy and support. They were Nora and Don Gerber and Nicki and John Pappas. Nora was suspected to have a chromosomal abnormality in her child, and they were talking about possible Down syndrome. Nicki was suspected to have a blood disorder called thalassemia in her child. These two couples were recommended to have advanced gene therapy as soon as possible.

They went to see the doctor at World Fertility and Genetic Clinic for further advice.

He took them in separately. First ones were Nora and Don Gerber.

"Doctor, please explain the situation for us to understand it better."

"Of course. Sometimes these things happen. It is not anyone's fault. Certainly it is not your fault. Normally every cell has a pair of

THE CLINIC

twenty-three chromosomes, making it a total of forty-six chromosomes. Sometimes the body at germinal stage misbehaves and makes an extra chromosome for some people. For some others, it makes one less chromosome. Either way, it makes the baby abnormal. When there is an extra chromosome on the twenty-first pair, it is called trisomy 21. These babies develop Down syndrome."

"What happens when the child has Down syndrome?"

"The child is mentally deficient with an IQ of 50. However, there are some children with Down syndrome who have completed high school and have even been gainfully employed."

"How often does this kind of birth occur?"

"According to statistics, it occurs in one out of one thousand normal births. The chances are higher when the mother's age is also higher."

"How does the child look with Down syndrome?"

"It has a flat face, slanting eyes, protruding tongue, larger ears, stunted growth, hearing and vision problems, small chin, umbilical hernia, and infertility."

"Is it a genetically inherited condition?"

"No, it is not inherited. It is not due to a genetic defect of the parents. It just happens for no reason."

"Do they live a normal life?"

"No. Their life expectancy is around sixty years. Many things go wrong by then, with cardiac, musculoskeletal, and neurological problems."

"Is the diagnosis by mother's blood test accurate?"

"No. It just gives us a suspicion. Further diagnosis can be confirmed by testing the amniotic fluid and sampling of chorionic villus from placenta."

"Are these tests dangerous?"

"Yes and no. They are done under ultrasound guidance. Sometimes it can result in injury to the fetus and even miscarriage. Generally they are safe procedures, however."

"What should we do if it is confirmed to be Down syndrome?"

"In Europe, 92 percent of parents opt for termination of pregnancy by abortion. In the US, 75 percent of parents also opt for termination of pregnancy. However, the other 25 percent do not want termination of pregnancy. Also, certain states do not permit such termination based on humanitarian and religious convictions."

"What problems do we encounter if we decide to raise the child?"

"It will be a big commitment to raise the child. Special attention, extra effort and work will be needed. Some send them to special schools, but some insist on sending them to regular schools. They will need constant help with every aspect of life."

"Is there any specific treatment available to cure this condition?"

"There is a possibility of undergoing a gene therapy before the child is born. It is experimental and not yet accepted by the scientific community."

"How do we go about undertaking that therapy instead of opting for abortion?"

"I can refer you to a special laboratory. It is a one-of-a-kind and only one such facility to my knowledge. It is affiliated with our World Fertility and Genetic Clinic. All our complex genetic issues are referred to them if our clients agree."

"Please tell us more about this place and how do we make an appointment."

"I shall talk to Nicki and John Pappas first and then go over details of this place to all four of you together."

Nicki and John had a separate private meeting.

"Your baby has the signs of having a blood disorder called thalassemia."

"What is that, doctor?"

"It is a type of anemia that is genetically inherited. It is likely that both of you are carriers, since you both have Mediterranean ancestry."

"We were in good health and did not have any symptoms."

"That is normal. You had only one mutation in each of you. That is why you did not have any symptoms."

"What happens to the baby once it is born?"

"It will be having anemia, and sometimes it can be severe. The baby may have stunted growth, weakness, facial deformity, heart problems, yellowish skin, enlarged spleen, and iron overload with metabolic problems."

"Can it be treated?"

"Yes, but only partially. It may need transfusions, intake of various medications such as hydroxyurea, folic acid, and sometimes bone marrow transplant."

"Is there a gene therapy I have heard of?"

"Yes. In one method, the child's blood is collected for hematopoietic stem cells (HSCs), and then it is treated with a b-globin gene using a lentiviral vector. Then the person is given chemotherapy to destroy the current bone marrow. Afterward, the newly treated HSCs are reinfused."

"How and when is this type of treatment done?"

"It is possible to do this while the baby is still in the womb."

"How is that possible?"

"The baby's blood is drawn from the umbilical cord, treated, and then reinfused, all done when the baby is still inside the womb."

"Wow. That is unbelievable."

They sounded astonished.

"Now that we are both carriers, is it possible to prevent it from happening to our next child?"

"Yes, a new method is being devised. During in-vitro fertilization, the embryos are checked immediately after fertilization to see if they have defective genes. Such ones are discarded. We select the embryos that do not have the defect and then we implant them in the uterus during the in-vitro fertilization."

"We would like to explore treating this child while being pregnant and also prevent a future child from getting the defect. What should we do?"

"For this child, I shall have to refer you to this best genetic center called World Genetic Research Laboratory. For the next child, we should do in-vitro fertilization, unlike natural pregnancy you had this time around."

"So tell us more about this center."

"I have another couple who may want to go to this center. I shall discuss more with all four of you together."

So he called all four for a group conference.

He went over some details.

"World Fertility and Genetic Clinic works closely with the World Genetic Research Laboratory to solve advanced genetic issues. The clinic is the front office, and the genetic laboratory is the back office."

"Where is it located?"

"It is located in an unidentified nameless island in the Caribbean Sea, hidden among several other unoccupied and deserted islands in the general area. This particular island has been named as the Lab Island."

"Please tell us more about this island."

"It is about ten miles long and five miles wide with shallow waters all around. The closest uninhabited island is about six miles away, and the closest country with an airport is Cuba. There is a helicopter pad on top of the building that houses the laboratory. It will take forty-five minutes of helicopter ride in the southeast direction from Cuba to reach there. The only other method of transportation is by speedboat, which is three hours of sailing from Cuba."

"Does that mean we have to go to Cuba first?"

"Yes. The trip has to be prearranged through Cuba as the transfer place."

"Who owns this laboratory?"

"No one really knows the ownership details. An anonymous dummy corporation purchased the island from another anonymous fake company ten years ago. The officers who signed for the deed are also fake names."

"Is it part of Cuba or some other country?"

"The island is not under jurisdiction of any nation, including the United States. It is in the international waters, does not have any records, affiliation, taxation, or regulation by anyone."

"Why do they maintain such high secrecy?"

"Secrecy and privacy are protected very much since the clients do not want it any other way. Many high-value clients seek their help for uncommon and unusual reasons."

"Why can't they do this work in a more legitimate place?"

"The type of work done is prohibited in all other nations, since it borders on legality, morality, and ethics. Human rights activists and moralists will make trouble for such work. Moreover, some of the clients are high-profile individuals, who want to maintain their strict privacy."

"If it is doing questionable activities, why is it being allowed to conduct such work?"

"Because such work is needed for advancement of science. Many such actions are also helping humanity. Many couple have benefited from the good results. The line between good and bad is very thin and depends upon the perception of the observer."

"How good is this laboratory?"

"It is one of the best we have in the entire world. They get the work done with no interference from any rules, laws, or government. The only thing they care about is client's satisfaction and getting the expected results."

"How well is it staffed?"

"They are well staffed. There are twenty full-time highly intelligent genetic scientists working in the laboratory. They have master's degree and doctorate degrees but chose to work here."

"If they are that well qualified, why do they work in this remote area?"

"They like it because of the opportunities to explore science beyond the norms that are not allowed in the civilized world. Some of them had serious legal problems or family issues in the past to the extent they cannot find work in regular workplaces. They now prefer to work in anonymous places. Moreover, they are provided with whatever equipment or supplies they need to conduct their research."

"What about other staff members?"

"There are forty assistants, and eighty lower-level workers to support these scientists. In addition, there are security guards, engineers, and maintenance workers."

"What amenities do they have here?"

"Accommodation and food are provided in the campus. Electricity is generated with a power generator, but there is no internet, no cell phones, no Wi-Fi."

"How good is their hospital?"

"A separate section of the building is occupied by an ultramodern hospital with full operating room and ICU facilities where they can perform advanced transplantation procedures. They also treat any medical problems for the residents in the island. Highly trained transplant surgeons, neurosurgeons, and other physicians work here, along with nurses and other paramedical staff. They perform standard medical procedures and also advanced experimental procedures."

"Where do they get patients from?"

"Other doctors or other fertility clinics refer almost all patients. They have to go through screening protocols on the internet web site. They must be willing to make the required payments and comply with the rules set by the World Genetic Research Laboratory."

"What types of research do they conduct?"

"One type of research done is genetic modifications to treat medical disorders, with the theme of 'genes instead of pills' to treat or prevent various medical problems. Disorders with proven gene therapy already include muscular dystrophy, retinal problems, neurological disorders, and congenital malformations. Genes for early detection and early treatment of cancers are being researched. The future also lies in increasing longevity and decreasing onset of Alzheimer's disease, dementia, and heart disease. Tay-Sachs disease is probably preventable with genetic manipulation.

"In your case, they can genetically rectify the trisomy 21 of your baby by removing the third chromosome from it and make it normal again. They can also cure thalassemia and sickle cell disease by one-time genetic therapy instead of lifelong medications. All of this is done while your baby is still your womb."

"What is the history in this type of science?"

"Thomas Hunt Morgan ushered modern genetics when physical basis of heredity was explained. Genetically transmitted disorders were discovered, such as Alkaptonuria (1902), albinism (1903), short finger (1905), cataract (1906), Huntington chorea (1913), Duchenne muscular dystrophy (1913), color blindness (1914), and hemophilia (1916). Genetic methods are used in creating vaccine against the coronavirus (COVID-19). It involves replacing one of the RNA of the virus with a spy RNA. This modified RNA is in the vaccine. When injected in the body, it thinks it is the real virus and makes the antibodies."

"Can gene therapy delay aging process?"

"Yes. Genetic research is done to delay aging process. There is a genetic code built inside of every living creature that determines the life expectancy of that creature. The genetic code is predetermined and can be called destiny or fate. For example, a housefly is slated to die in thirty-five days, while a sequoia tree can live for two thousand years. Humans are expected to live for one hundred years. Aging and elderly status are of major concerns for all. Everyone would like to stay healthy as long as possible. Everyone wants to delay the eventuality of death. Everyone would like to delay aging process and live longer. The true answer is with the genes."

"How do the genes affect aging?"

"Aging goes through a process that is genetically controlled. At the very beginning of life, a single cell is able to become any type of organ. After birth, they grow in size and volume but do not make new organs. Further later in life, they are coded to replace lost or worn-out cells. Still later, the cells are unable to repair themselves and progressively deteriorate, and the body dies. The theory is that by modifying the genetic code, one can delay aging and age-related illnesses. Such genetic treatment can be marketed for one to $2 million for a single patient. Obviously, the profits are enormous."

"What other types of gene technology is being done?"

"Another type of research done in the laboratory is gene editing and cloning. These trials have been done on animal models and on cellular materials so far. Cloning of humans and gene editing to create designer babies in humans have been banned by all countries and are considered illegal and unethical. However, the power of people's minds cannot be changed. The desire to have their own bodies living forever is an overwhelming ambition and dream."

"How is cloning used to benefit the person?"

"One method is to clone their own bodies, keep these bodies in a secured area to be used for harvesting and replacing diseased organs of the owner. The newly created cloned body is sacrificed as donors to benefit the owners to replace their worn-out heart, lungs, kidneys, bones, and other tissues as needed. Many more of such cloned bodies can be manufactured if necessary. Yet another choice is to allow the newly cloned body to live and take over all functions of the owner as the owner dies of old age. The cloned child is going to be identical to the owner unlike a normally born child."

"Are there any other experimentations going on there?"

"Another major experimentation in the laboratory is about brain and its functions. Elon Musk, the billionaire entrepreneur, is conducting research on pigs by implanting microcomputers in their brain to see if they can be modulated. A similar experimentation needs to be done on humans to treat several of the neurological disorders.

"Brain transplantation is a possibility in the future. This will be of help to those young people who have a healthy body but are suddenly brain-dead following an automobile accident or a gunshot wound or even brain cancers. Transplantation of heart, lungs, liver, kidneys, skin, face, limbs, intestine, and pancreas are being done regularly. So why not brain transplantation? What better place to conduct the experiment other than this laboratory, using unwanted humans as guinea pigs."

"Do they do any DNA-related work for solving crimes?"

"DNA analysis is a big business by itself. The laboratory provides assistance to private detectives, organizations, and governments on analysis of DNA and genetic information on individuals for a price. This is called forensic genetics. Items tested include blood, saliva, semen, and hair and any other tissues such as skin, bone, teeth, urine, feces, and items touched by the person such as chewing gum, cigarette butts, toothbrush, and even earwax. Skin cells can be clinging to anything touched by the suspect. A tiny drop of blood has numerous white blood cells, and each nucleus of a white blood cell contains the person's entire genome."

"Can you give some examples by which DNA analysis helped solve crimes?"

"Link can be created between the person and DNA of animals or plants to provide circumstantial evidence of the crime. For example, during a certain murder, both one person and a dog were shot. The dog's blood splattered on the shirt of the suspected murderer. Investigators were able to connect this particular dog's blood on his shirt, and this resulted in his conviction. Similarly in another case, the suspect stepped on dog feces, and the shoe had the matched feces on DNA analysis. In another case, the rape victim's dog urinated on the attacker's vehicle, leading to conviction. In another instance, a certain rare desert plant that grows only in a certain location had its seeds noticed in the pickup truck of the suspect, proving the presence of that person in that location, where the dead body was found, further proven by DNA analysis of the seed and the plant."

"What other research do they do?"

"One of the groundbreaking researches done in the World Genetic Research Laboratory is creating new life out of chemicals, just as God did it many millions of years ago. First step was in creating new virus out of simple chemicals, since the structure of the virus is simple. Next, it has been moved up in creating bacteria."

"How do they get samples for these experiments?"

"In order to conduct such studies, one has to obtain cell samples from those with old age and terminal illnesses, modify the genes from these samples, inject them back into those individuals in incremental doses, and study the effect of such effort.

"One modality is to obtain blood and tissue samples from nursing home patients all over the world with dementia or Alzheimer's disease. They are then transported to the laboratory for analysis and gene modification, and the prepared medicine is injected back into those patients. They are further studied in the nursing homes as to their behavior. This is human experimentation and will be considered as unethical, illegal. The Fertility and Genetic Clinic maintains relationship with a number of nursing homes in mainland USA as well as in other countries. There are a large number of patients left to die in these nursing homes by their own families. The main goal is to know if their life can be prolonged or their quality of life improved."

"What about cancer treatments?"

"Then there are those individuals who had metastatic cancers who have been treated with surgery, chemotherapy, radiation therapy, and now facing terminal situation. Often they are under hospice care or in nursing homes. But their tissue and blood samples are of value to study their gene abnormalities. It is estimated that $50 billion are at stake for genetic testing and gene treatment for cancers."

"We heard that aborted tissues are used for genetic experiments?"

"Newborn babies and aborted fetuses provide gold mines of blood and tissues to harvest stem cells, embryonic multipotent cells, and culture materials to make new tissues. Connection with abortion clinics and maternity hospitals across the globe can provide huge resources. The materials are transported to the laboratory or drug companies to process them further."

"It seems they have their own resources in plenty."

"In addition to the abovementioned workers, there are several humans and animals kept in captivity for genetic research. These individuals were brought here through human trafficking methods. There are hundreds of people who are unwanted by the society, and they disappear with no trace all the time. No one looks for them and no one cares about them. But they are very valuable for the genetic laboratory for live human experiments and research. Such research will not be permitted under any circumstances anywhere else. One may call it the Frankenstein's place."

"Why do these brilliant scientists prefer to work here?"

"World Genetic Research Laboratory offers a paradise, a fantastic working place for the scientists with no rules or regulations. Dreams can fly and imaginations can take off with no limits. Many of the scientists are known for rouge activities in their own countries. They are paid extremely well beyond what they can dream of in their homelands. No expenses are curtailed for the research. Raw materials are always available. Humans and animals are kept captive for experimentation or sacrifice at short notice. All protocols and methodology are up to the scientist at the World Genetic Research Laboratory."

"No wonder they like it here."

"It is a dream world for the pure scientist."

"How long do these experiments take to complete?"

THE CLINIC

"These can take many years of labor and discipline. The results of their work depend on lifetime evaluation of the subjects. The eventual outcome is still unknown."

"These experiments must be very expensive."

"These experiments cost huge amounts of time, effort, and resources. Without large capital commitment by individuals or corporations, it cannot be done. Obviously, those who are investing in such laboratories need some returns for themselves."

"Are they doing these experiments illegally and without ethics?"

"There are many sides to this viewpoint. Much depends upon how one looks at it. When taking part in a crime or wrongdoing conducted by another person, knowingly or unknowingly, the second person becomes an accomplice to a crime and can be found guilty of being an accessory to the crime. The same applies for moral and ethical principles in genetic research.

"HESC (human embryonic stem cell research) is inherently problematic. It is not the same as doing such studies on plants or animals. Aborted embryos are used to obtain the embryonic stem cells. Can it be a reason to conduct illegal abortion for nonmedical reasons and for profit-making? Supernumerary embryos produced in the course of IVF are destroyed—is that murder of newborns? Is it likely to lead to selection of the unborn? Do these embryos have a right to live like other zygotes?

"In commercial or industrial research, many trials and errors occur. Many incomplete or even completed products are abandoned. Many near-perfect products are discarded for quality control. If that is applied to HESC, is it morally right to kill many unborn? Is embryo research a morally evil process by its very nature and, therefore, should not be permitted?

"If we can allow genetic makeup of agricultural products for increasing productivity, increasing size and color of the produce, and selectively plant certain cash crops instead of naturally grown weeds, who are we to say that we cannot do the same to humans? When we genetically modified rice and wheat to harvest larger crops, we called it green revolution and adored it as a solution to reduce starvation. We encourage chicken farms and cattle farms with the plan to kill them, to increase their meat size, to increase the milk production, and we create fishponds to supply restaurants with choice fish year-round, and we selectively inseminate cows and horses to make better breeds out of them. Why not humans too? God created all living beings. Who gave the humans the right to genetically modify them but not to ourselves to make better humans?

"In the field of gene therapy, many new discoveries are being made to treat various illnesses that had no cure, many inherited conditions are explained based on genetic background, and many illnesses are prevented with early intervention. So it has its good side and bad side. Conflicts between bioscience, biopolitics, and biolaws have origins in religious, economic, social, ethnic, and moral considerations.

"When Zika virus rapidly spread across South and Central America in 2016, it caused nearly one thousand children to be born with birth defects and microcephaly. The virus was spreading through a mosquito. Using the gene technology, the breed of mosquitos was eliminated, thus controlling the Zika outbreak. Genetically modified mosquitoes are being used to kill Aedes aegypti mosquitoes, which is responsible for transmission of many viral infections such as dengue, Chikungunya, and malaria. That is helping humans."

Everyone became speechless and silent.

Chapter 8

The Website

Nora and Don Gerber and Nicki and John Pappas were astounded and speechless after hearing the work and experimentations going on at the World Genetic Research Laboratory. They were hesitant to some degree. Should we go there or not?

The doctor asked them, "What are you planning to do? Time is of the essence here to make a decision."

"Can you please summarize the options?"

"Yes, you have basically three choices—first is to terminate the pregnancy. If this is your choice, you have to do it immediately, probably by tomorrow."

"Why? What is the rush?"

"It is already thirteen weeks now. Your gene test was done at twelve weeks of pregnancy. Before the legalists and moralists get to know, it must be terminated. The longer you wait, the more difficult it will be."

"What is the second choice?"

"You continue with the pregnancy and have the baby delivered at full term. You will have to deal with the disability of the child as you go along."

"And the final choice?"

"You go to the Lab Island for genetic therapy."

"What is the next step if we decide to go to this place that you recommend?"

"First step is to have the genetic defect confirmed. This will need an amniocentesis at the minimum. For Nora, we would recommend a placental chorionic biopsy in addition, since her treatment is going to be more difficult."

"Okay. When do we do this?"

"Your treatment at the Lab Island must be scheduled to take place around twenty-four weeks of pregnancy when the baby is grown up but not ready for delivery yet."

"What else needs to be done ahead of time?"

"Then you have to be enrolled as a patient member of the website, also known as DWS."

"Pease tell us more about this website."

"It is named DWS, which stands for Deep Whale Surfing. It also means Dark Web Site for the way it is functioning."

"Who owns it or runs it?"

"No one knows who owns it, who manages it, or who is downloading material into it. But it functions extremely well and efficiently. It reaches the entire world with no barriers. The materials posted for customers are accurate, dependable, and current."

"How can you open it?"

"It can be opened only by authorized individuals. General public cannot open it. It is only for members and employees and clients through separate portals and separate logins."

"How do patients who seek treatment at the World Genetic Research Laboratory get to register and go through the website?"

"Yes, patients and clients who need services have a separate portal, different from employees and members. However, the referring doctor from a member organization has to enlist them for that specific treatment."

The doctor told them that he would have to initiate enlisting the Gerber and Pappas families into the website if they wanted to proceed further. There was an advance token fee involved for downloading their information and medical records and registering for their care online. Once it was activated, they could open their personal sections to follow directions and ask questions.

Nora and Nicki agreed.

"Let us go ahead and plan for the genetic treatment of the baby."

The doctor said, "I must warn you that there will be no guarantee as to the outcome. The baby may end up with a premature delivery. Payments must be made ahead of time in installments."

"But this appears to be the best course of action, between terminating the pregnancy and doing nothing. Let us try and see if we can correct it. If it did not work, we are back to square one."

While waiting, they wanted to know more about the website. They were curious about the name DWS and its functioning. They were referred to Melissa Sarkowsky, an employee member of DWS. She had to enter her business data on the website from time to time, but she was not a customer member or a client member of DWS, and she could not open their sections of the website.

Melissa replied, "I am not a regular member myself. I have access only to the employee portal, since I work for the sperm bank. But as far as I know, the regular membership is by invitation and referrals only and not for anyone and everyone."

"So what are the requirements to become a regular member?"

"As I understand, the requirements are strict. It is only for the big shots. Members must be holding influential positions in government offices, corporations, or organizations in any country. They must have a net worth of at least $10 million. They must have demonstrated celebrity status in sports, arts, politics, or academics. They must be willing to comply with the strict rules and regulations of the website."

"Is there a fee to join?"

"First time initiation fee is $10,000. Then there is an annual fee of $1,000."

"Why is the fee so high and why do they have such restrictions? What do they get out of it?"

"I am told that the rewards are good. Information obtained is highly valuable, secretive, and tailored to needs of individual members. There are rare opportunities that only the elite can dream of. They are deals of a lifetime with huge profits."

"Okay, let us say someone is ready to join. What do they have to do next?'

"An application form needs to be filled out initially, giving all the contact information, date of birth, designation, past and present jobs, and net worth. The masterminds of the DWS will conduct their own independent research and track them down from past to present and assess their future goals and ambitions."

"How do they maintain the security of the site?"

"Login to the site requires three layers of security. First is use of personal ID and password as in any other online transaction. Then there are three secret security questions that must be answered correctly with only one chance. After that, there is a fingerprint recognition, face recognition, voice recognition, and eye (retina) recognition. Then a one-time login code number will be texted, which must be entered within two minutes. If any of these is incorrect or unacceptable, the website will shut down automatically for the next twelve hours. The site will open only after these personal identifications are completed."

"Does the website track you?"

"The site tracks every single detail once it is opened. It knows who opened it, when and where it was opened, what was searched, what was purchased, what was reviewed, and what were the interests of the member. It remembers everything and automatically brings up topics of interest, deals, opportunities, and other items that are not available to the public. Once you are a member, you are part of the DWS club. Direct communication from the DWS to the member is very limited and only when a deal is in the offing. There is no direct communication allowed between the members of DWS."

"Is it expensive to buy stuff from this website?"

"There is a price for everything, but it is the final outcome and benefit to the customer that matters and not the money. It is the result that matters and not the methods. It may be illegal, immoral, criminal, and unethical, but if it gets you the result, then it is worth it."

"Give me some examples."

"Look at some of the rare opportunities one can only dream of. Let us talk about winning an election—how to get dirt on the opponent, how to find weakness of the opponent, arrange for fake news in social media about the opponent, arrange for WikiLeaks on past correspondences that were supposed to be classified, know about health of the opponent or family members, find out their vulnerable habits and addictions, discover their campaign strategies, and, in certain instances, arrange to eliminate the opponent by accidents, poisoning, or murder."

"What about business deals?"

"You can find ways to outdo your competition in a corporate warfare. Arrange for an insider spy, find out about their strategies, get to know about their new products, vulnerable habits of the CEO or other top officials, hack their computers, lure their key employees to work for your company, and so forth."

"What else for a person's benefit?"

"Look at other possibilities and services—you can find a safe way to murder someone with no trace, you can make 300-percent profit in a short-term deal, you want a high-class hooker to work on you discreetly to satisfy your fantasies, buy human slaves, create gene-edited babies, get organs for transplantation without any waiting time, arrange for terror attacks, or buy and sell large-scale ammunition."

"In this digital world, anything can be done from remote location. Any computer can be hacked. Any information can be obtained. Anyone can be contacted and enticed to work for you without that person's knowledge. Anyone can be manipulated. It is the end result that matters, not the methods or means."

"How do these things work? Who is the one hacking it and why?"

"Cybersecurity is a major concern for all businesses and corporations. Hacking is a lucrative work. Just the fear of being hacked or threat of leaking their data is adequate for many companies to pay up the demand. Covert digital operations and hackings are authorized by every government to sabotage enemy countries in various ways. They are used in election manipulations, shutting down nuclear plants, shutting down electric grids, shutting down oil pipelines, conducting illegal arms trades and drug trades, and terrorist activities. It is a tool in modern warfare. Dark websites help international criminal activities that benefit crooks. Money, sex, human trafficking, drug trafficking, arms deals, political and judicial power, racist activities, and power and control are all in play."

"That is for governments. What about industries?"

"As use of technology increases in day-to-day life, as more and more people are working from home and from remote locations, and as dependence on digital technology pervades every sector of the society, including large and small financial transactions, health care, transportation and travels, communication between individuals and organizations, then the risk of leak, loss of data, and malfunction of the entire systems become a real threat.

"A number of industries are vulnerable and at risk. Small firms and individuals are unprepared and can be attacked the most. When a wrong button is clicked on the laptop, the hacker can take control of the entire computer and hack all personal and financial information, leading to blackmail, swindling, and embezzlement and extortion."

"What is the so-called ransomware?"

"Ransomware is a regular phenomenon when the firms decide to pay up the ransom rather than take the risk of breach of their data. According to a survey by WSJ Pro research, 40 percent of the companies would pay a ransom rather than report to police or FBI. Construction industry responded that 74 percent of them would pay a ransom, and 57 percent of technology industry would do so. For them, the breach of data is most consequential. At times, there is an insider or black sheep willing to work with the hackers either for revenge or monetary gains."

"What about regular people like us?"

"We are taking huge number of pictures and videos more than ever and are making digital communications in personal, professional, casual, and social settings more than ever with the easy availability of cell phone, cameras, and social media outfits such as Facebook, Twitter, FaceTime, Zoom, Google, and WhatsApp. We think we can delete them, but often we end up downloading them into the social media platforms that go viral all over the world. This becomes fodder for the cybercriminals and extortionists. Remote working and working from home that has increased due to coronavirus pandemic has put security at risk. People do not realize how much of their personal information they are revealing to the public through their pictures—of their house, family, friends, hobbies, habits, travels, pictures, art, work, and office. In the process, they provide clues about their date of birth, age, address, passwords, and usernames, permitting the hackers to zero in."

"Wow."

"Discovery of a sophisticated malware called Stuxnet in 2010 was a milestone in cyber warfare. It was used to sabotage the Iranian nuclear facilities conducted by the US and Israel. The use of computer-based digital virus as a weapon instead of conventional military actions was very effective. The danger is that similar attacks are possible by terrorists and rogue countries, which can do the same to paralyze electrical grid, transportation networks, airport control, financial system, and so forth. Cyber warfare is called the fifth domain after land, sea, air, and space. In 2017, international malware attack called NotPetya was conducted by Russian military."

"Can they hack Twitter accounts?"

"Twitter accounts of several prominent individuals such as Obama, Biden, Elon Musk, and several others were hacked. It was not clear if it was an outsider such as Russia or an insider from Twitter who did it for monetary gains. Russia tried to steal coronavirus vaccine being developed in the US by cyber hack."

"What is phishing?"

"Phishing occurs when a hacker entices a user to disclose passwords and user ID and other account information by luring them into a financial reward. The user is enticed to send the information to a fake website that looks very legitimate on the electronic screen. It is called social engineering."

"Is there a person or specific groups of people who do the hacking?"

"I have heard the name Wang Zon, a Chinese guy who is in charge. But he must be having many associates in different parts of the world, including Russia, India, Africa, and South America. Often they are teenagers who are working in slum areas, keeping a low profile. But they are paid well. Keep in mind that many companies pay up just on threat of hacking. We are told the average pay-up is $250,000 for each threat."

"How do the members benefit from joining this club?"

"Members of the DWS can request a certain task to be accomplished, and the site can do it or facilitate it for the right price or compensation. It could be money or a return favor. Such high-value personalized services cannot be obtained by ordinary means. It is like a mafia king. You pay a price, and a job will be done."

"Who runs the DWS and who are the brains behind it?"

"Again no one knows who is in charge of the DWS, but it works well and does the job. One Indian IT specialist by the name Ravi Sitaram is considered to be one of the brains behind. But I am sure that there must be many more such people who work part-time or full-time for the DWS. Thomas Goodguy is another person higher up in the organization. He is the one who helped me get this job.

"Sometimes people do not even know that they are working for the DWS, but they think they are working on a job for some multinational firm. It is suspected that there is an international underground consortium that manages it. There are many unknown locations around the globe, and there are thousands of engineers and computer specialists working on them. An army of high-IQ individuals guides the work. They are independent of any country or company. They work for themselves and spend the money on latest equipment and research. They are always two steps ahead of the known scientific progress to the rest of the world. They are also paid very well. Any breach of internal rules and confidentiality will be met with severe punishment, including death."

"Tell me more about DWS."

"The underworld leaders as well as major corporations of the globe have a role in running the DWS. Politicians and governments want to use it, and at the same time, they want to condemn it. Everyone wants to destroy it, and at the same time, everyone wants to preserve it. They want to denounce it and at the same time utilize it. No one person is in charge, but input is coming from all sorts of sources for the same goal to advance research, to deliver services, and to do things that no one or no country can do openly. There is a con-

THE CLINIC

stantly revolving group of leaders from the international consortium who declare that only actions matter and results matter and not the person or pride."

Chapter 9

The Travel

Nora and Don Gerber as well as Nicki and John Pappas decided to explore their options and chances at the World Genetic Research Laboratory jointly. They decided to support each other and help each other. One of them looked up the travel details to Cuba, another one studied the website called DWS, another one talked to the doctor at World Fertility and Genetic Clinic to make the referral.

Once the referral was made into the system, they were able to log into the website and get further instructions and directions after making the initial down payment. They filled out all the details requested in the questionnaire. First, they have to go to Cuba and then take the helicopter ride.

"I am a little bit scared to go through Cuba, being a communist country," said Nora.

"It should be fairly safe as long as we get proper permits both from the US and Cuba," replied John.

All this had to be scheduled and paid in full ahead of the trip. The US permit to travel back and forth was needed. They were to obtain the permit from both the US and Cuba under medically needy category.

The flight from New York to Havana was uneventful. They had to stay overnight in a hotel there. The amenities were meager by US standards, but it was considered as a good hotel over there. They got a chance to see the effect of communist rule for the past fifty or more years. Poverty and lack of developments were visible all around.

THE CLINIC

The helicopter ride was the scary part with the ride over the sea. It was not easy to recognize the specific island from the air, but the pilot knew his whereabout. The chopper landed on a helipad on top of a high-rise building. As they stepped out, a uniformed nurse and an administrator were ready to receive them with a welcoming smile. An elevator took them down to the main floor, where they were checked in, registered, and taken to their quarters. Nora tried to call her family, and John tried to check his emails. They found out that there was no Wi-Fi in the building and that no outside contacts could be made.

Due to prior registration on the website, referral letters from the World Fertility and Genetic Clinic and prepayments, everything seemed smooth. They felt at ease. They were given a brief tour of the facility and were given food and beverages.

In the morning the next day, they had appointment to meet the doctors and genetic scientists. So they were told to rest and relax. No television, no cell phone, no internet, and no social media. Have early dinner and go to sleep. They slept well, since they had a long day and were tired.

After breakfast, they met with the doctor separately. The message was the same: "We shall do our best, but we cannot guarantee the results. No one in the world has the ability to do what we do here. This is the most advanced and freelance genetic center, where we can do what the customer wants us to do. You have really nothing to lose by trying. If we fail, then you are back to square one as you started. But if we win, you have achieved a great deal for yourself and your child. Irrespective of the outcome, the payments must be made in full before we start the therapy."

They signed the required paperwork and had already made the payments. The ladies were taken into separate rooms. The men had free time to wander around and walk. That was when John met his old schoolmate in the cafeteria and Don ran into his family friend in the hallway.

"Hey. Surprised to meet you here of all places."

"Unbelievable. What are you doing here?"

"We are here as patients or clients as you like to call us. Our wives are having some sort of genetic treatments."

"What a surprise."

"We have some free time. Can you give us a tour of this strange place in a remote island?"

"Oh sure. We have only limited time since we have work to do. But we can meet later at lunchtime in the cafeteria."

"Okay then. See you at lunch."

Over that day and the next few days, they learned quite a lot about this island and the genetic research laboratory through these friends.

Chapter 10

The Creation

During the next five days, Don and John had plenty of free time to explore the World Genetic Research Laboratory and had a lot of conversations with their friends. They gathered a lot of information, since there was nothing else to do in this lonely place. No cell phone, no television, no newspapers, and no outside contact.

"Tell us about one outstanding research being done at this center."

"Scientists working at the World Genetic Research Laboratory have one big ambition, and that is to create new life out of chemicals. It is a challenge, but it did happen many million years ago with the right combination of energy, environment, and chemicals. Can we recreate life de novo in the laboratory? This is a dream work for the bioscientists all over the world. Man wants to be God? Only God can create life as far as all the teachings go. Bioscientists have come from all over the world to this island laboratory just to participate in this work, which is impossible anywhere else. They have free hand and excellent amenities to do their research without any interruptions or bureaucracy."

"Do they use certain chemicals?"

"Deoxyribonucleic acid or called DNA for short is the basis of life. Every living being on this planet has DNA, which stores the genetic information in it. It is needed to create the species, transmit it to next generation, grow it, and maintain it. It is the blueprint, it is the microchip, it is the computer, and it is the magic wand that makes everything in life happen."

"Where is the DNA stored in the body?"

"When one dissects deeper into the body, it is the cells that make up the tissues. There are fifty trillion cells in a human body. The cells are made up of chromosomes, which in turn are made up of DNA. But then the DNA is made up of a few chemicals held together with the help of a few other chemicals. Each DNA molecule contains thousands and thousands of copies of four specific nitrogen-rich bases called as adenine (A), guanine (G), cytosine (C) and thymine (T). So it is these chemicals, with the help of additional enzymes and deoxyribose sugars and phosphates, that make up life. Why can't we put these blotches of chemicals in a test tube and create life in the test tube? Simple as it sounds, it has been an impossible dream."

"How was the very first life created in this universe?"

"It did not come automatically out of nowhere for sure. Life as we see today can be in the form of minute particles as bacteria or as huge organisms like the elephants. There must have been a setup or scenario when the inorganic chemicals came together in the presence of energy from the sun or thermonuclear explosions at the time of the origin of the planet Earth. Multiple different forms of lives emerged with proper amounts of water, temperature, and other unknown requirements. Once life formed, they procreated, mutated, some perished forever, some survived and continue to exist."

"So where do we scientists stand today in their efforts to create new life de novo in a laboratory, simulating the conditions at the origin of planet Earth?"

"On May 19, 2017, the British news magazine *Guardian* Science Edition reported that scientists at Cambridge University had created the world's first living organism, which had a synthetic and altered DNA code. This lab had created a new strain of a well-known bacterium called E. coli, which is commonly found in the soil and inside human gut. The artificial genome is 970 pages long on full-size paper and took over two years to create. The new bug was called Syn 61. It was a little longer than the E. coli and grew more slowly.

THE CLINIC

The scientists initially edited the original genome of E. coli, and after eighteen thousand edits, the redesigned genome was chemically synthesized, which was then placed inside the old E. coli to replace the original genome."

"What else has been done?"

"Efforts to create new life have been an ongoing research topic for scientists all across the globe, costing billions and billions of dollars. On July 28, 2017, STAT website described the efforts as 'chemicals to life' from Netherlands, Germany, Japan and China. In the USA, a program called Build a Cell was started under Caltech/Stanford University guidance. Scripps Institute in La Jolla produced a modified strain of E. coli using synthetic DNA. Afterward, a Harvard professor by the name George Church opened the George Church Institute of Regenesis in China in collaboration with Chinese BGI for creating artificial life-forms."

"So what has your lab done so far?"

"The World Genetic Research Laboratory has been working on creating a virus as the first step in creating life. Viruses have only RNA and do not need a full complex of DNA and do not need a full cell. DNA is a double helix, whereas RNA is simpler with only one chain. They were able to put together the required chemicals in various setups and incubate them, hoping for their growth and multiplication. It was extremely important to keep them contained, since no one knew the effects of these viruses in the human body if they invaded into a person. Security and safety-keeping the new virus strains were given extreme attention and importance."

"Are the viruses used for biological warfare?"

"One of the objectives of creating the virus is for biological warfare with other countries or for terrorist activities. The price for the virus is astronomical. Countries would pay handsome money to keep them stored for a biological warfare if necessary."

"Is it true that some viruses escaped from a lab and caused a worldwide pandemic?"

"It is possible that some of the workers in the laboratory can get infected with the new virus and unknowingly transmits it to several others. A similar incident happened when the coronavirus, also known as COVID-19, came out of a research laboratory in China. Within a short time of five months, it spread to the entire world, killing nearly one million people. The new virus strain turned out to be virulent, was constantly mutating itself, and caused unprecedented harm to the entire globe. Most countries had to go on lockdown for weeks, stopping every economic and trade activity, plunging the world into darkness as never seen before. Travel came to a standstill, people could not go anywhere, since they were forced into isolation and quarantine as if in house arrest. All restaurants and entertainments closed, schools and universities were shut down, and many offices were closed permanently. Several organizations and companies declared bankruptcy. Communication was by phone or by digital media. Hospitals were flooded with sick patients, elective medical and surgical cares were postponed, and visitors were not allowed to see their sick family members. Those in the hospitals died alone, with family not allowed to see them even after death. Funerals were held secretly. Morgues were full, and dead bodies were left in trucks for days together for wanting a disposal decision."

Chapter 11

The Disorders

They continued the interesting conversation on treating disorders and cancers using genetic technology.

"Is it possible that cancers are due to genetic mutations of certain cells? If so, can we treat cancers by gene manipulations?"

"How else can we explain the uncontrolled growth of these cells, which then become tumors and then spread to different parts of the body? If that is the case, one of the answers for treating or preventing cancers could be through gene therapy."

"How about studying the blood and body parts of people with advanced cancers and find a clue as to their genetic makeup?"

"Yes, it is being done. They are calling it liquid biopsy. Blood tests can show signs of cancer in certain cases."

"How about cancer screening by gene technology?"

"The simplest of the tasks is risk assessment for cancers. Doing BRCA-1 or BRCA-2 can assess breast cancer risk. It is not for everyone, since the result can lead into confusing recommendations. Hence, it is done only for those at high risk, with strong family history of breast cancers. Colon cancer can be detected early by doing DNA analysis on the stool. Some of the colon cancers and ovarian cancers are familial and are genetically transmitted."

"How does cancer kill a person?"

"That is an interesting question. In general, cancers have uncontrolled growth of cells in one spot and cause formation of a tumor. Often this tumor causes compression of tissues and organs with resultant aftereffects that can result in serious consequences."

"Give me an example."

"A tumor growth on the head of pancreas causes compression of the bile duct, resulting in jaundice and liver failure. A growth in the spinal cord causes paralysis of the body. A growth inside the brain causes death."

"What about the spread of the cancer?"

"That is also a factor. The cancer can spread to other areas from the original site. The new spots can cause damage by the same fashion."

"Any other way they can cause damage to the body?"

"The cancerous growth can cause blockage of tubular organ such as intestines, bile duct, ureters, or they can cause internal bleeding from their ulcerated surfaces."

"What about blood cancers?"

"Various blood cancers and lymphatic cancers can cause damage to bone marrow or cause dysfunction of the whole body system."

"What other progress is being made at this center besides cancer therapy?"

"World Genetic Research Laboratory is conducting experimental work in different health-care areas through genetics. They do the testing for various congenital or inherited disorders, risk assessment for cancers, risk assessment for premature death or neurological disorders, and such various medical problems and advise the patients and doctors. Several big biotech companies listed in the stock market have made huge returns and profits in short periods of one year or less."

"Will gene testing become popular before people get married?"

"Currently many young prospective brides and grooms undergo medical examination and blood tests to ensure that they do not carry any contagious diseases. In the future, a genetic testing will be done routinely as a premarital mandate. In the future, rules will be passed in many different countries that both the bride and the bridegroom must subject themselves for genetic evaluation to know if they carry any traits or inherited disorders. If such defective genes are identified, then their newborn babies will be subjected to genetic corrections so that they do not carry those disorders forward nor die young."

"What other types of gene testings are being done here?"

"They are also conducting advanced research in gene editing, transplantation, stem cell therapy, and gene sequencing as well as prolonging longevity through genetic manipulations."

"Have you had specific patients who were treated here? Tell us about their stories."

"Dora Smith and Don Picker met in college and fell in love. Both were Caucasians of Northern European ancestry and wanted to get married. Afterward, when they visited their family members, they came to know that some of their cousins had died at younger age due to recurrent lung infections and asthma. They did not think anything about it then. They started their family life together and were very thrilled when she became pregnant. A beautiful baby girl was born in a normal way. They started noticing some problems with the baby. Initially, she had episodes of constipation, and the stool afterward would be foul-smelling and greasy. When they hugged and kissed her, she would taste salty. After some time, they noticed she was not gaining weight as expected. Routine visit to her pediatrician revealed there might be some problem for growth and development.

"The doctor ordered certain blood tests and told them she has a condition called cystic fibrosis. The doctor also suggested genetic testing of both parents and warned them of the potential for various medical problems particularly with breathing and coughing issues. The parents wanted a second opinion, which confirmed the same. The parents were devastated. True enough, in a short while, she started having recurrent lung infections, thick mucous on coughing spells, and difficulty in breathing. They were on high alert to provide her with constant medical care with the knowledge that she might die at a young age.

"They realized that this is due to a genetic defect with a gene called CFTR. There is no treatment except for supportive care. This is when they heard about the World Genetic Research Laboratory. They wanted to know if her gene could be corrected at this time. While they were not able to give any assurances, they were willing to give it a try. They also offered to correct the gene of their next child upon conception and have the modified zygote reimplanted in the mother's womb as an in-vitro fertilization."

"That is really amazing. Tell us about another story."

"Robert James was nine years old and a good student in the class. That is when he started experiencing difficulty in seeing the writings by the teacher on the chalkboard. He was able to read his book and notes on his book. This situation progressively got worse. Slowly he moved to the back end of the class, since he was afraid of the teacher asking questions. He started relying on bigger and bigger print on his electronic devices to catch up with the lessons. Sensing something wrong, the teacher contacted his parents and wanted him to have eye examination by doctors.

"After various tests and advanced evaluations, the eye doctors came up with a diagnosis of Leber's congenital amaurosis (LCA). Both the parents and the boy were bewildered with the strange words and descriptions. They came to know that this is a genetic disorder affecting the retina and that there is no effective treatment. He will progressively lose total vision by the age twenty and will become totally blind. The information and warning was dire and disheartening.

"After advanced research and consultations, they came to know that gene therapy has been the only hope so far. A modified and genetically mutated adenovirus is used for gene therapy by researchers in the university. Injection of the genetic drug into the eye gave partial return of vision to the children that were treated this way. That is when they decided to go to World Genetic Research Laboratory for more advanced gene therapy. They had to pay one million dollars, but Robert got near-normal vision back on a permanent basis with no need for any further therapies. It was worth it for him."

"We heard about muscular disorders being treated?"

"Median life expectancy of a child born with congenital muscular dystrophy is fourteen to twenty-seven years. One type of it is called Duchenne muscular dystrophy (DMD). Patients experience muscle weakness, poor motor control, inability to stand or sit, scoliosis, foot deformities, difficulty in swallowing and in breathing, and chronic pain. The problem is a genetic disorder that is classified as autosomal recessive—in other words, two copies of the defective gene acquired one from each parent. The defect affects muscle proteins and makes them inefficient in its normal functions.

"At present, there is no effective treatment. A certain gene therapy is found to be promising that can cure the condition. The World Genetic Research Laboratory has multiple pathways to cure the disease. In addition to gene therapy for the affected child, they can also modify the gene of the parents as well as the newborn before birth inside the uterus. The children treated successfully by gene therapy can expect a normal life as any other person."

"Any treatment to increase life span?"

"Progeria, otherwise known as Hutchinson-Gilford syndrome, is a genetic disorder where one single gene is misplaced. The child looks completely normal at birth but ages rapidly and dies by age fourteen. It is not an inherited disorder, and so far there is no cure. The child has the look of large baldhead with prominent eyes and general weakness. The gene affected is called LMNA gene that codes for lamin A protein, which affects the muscles and growth. Experimental studies in mouse have shown promising results by correcting the specific gene using new gene technology."

"Any other congenital neurological problems?"

"Tay-Sachs disease is another genetic disorder, more prevalent among Ashkenazi Jews of Eastern European origin. A certain enzyme called hexosaminidase A is deficient, which is needed for breakdown of fatty substances. Thus, the fatty substance called gangliosides accumulates in the brain and nerve cells, causing their destruction. The child looks normal at birth but fails to turn, crawl, or sit by six months, which is when the diagnosis becomes evident. There is progressive loss of muscle control, blindness, paralysis, and recurrent pneumonia, which leads to death by age five. There could be seizures, and a classical cherry red spot is seen in the eyes. There is no cure at this time. Only symptomatic and supportive care is given. However, gene therapy to correct the defective gene is found very promising."

"Any condition that occurs in adults?"

"Amyloidosis is a condition that affects the liver and causes progressive liver damage due to the accumulation of the material called amyloid. Treatment has been ineffective till now. However, a company called Intellia came up with a new revolutionary gene therapy. One single injection through the vein using the CRISPR modality caused 87-percent reduction of the material called serum transthyretin, thus providing a near cure for a type of amyloidosis called transthyretin amyloidosis (ATTR). This caused excitement in the medical world, and the stock price of the Intellia Company almost doubled within one week."

"It seems to be a very amazing type of work being done here. Are they making big money?"

"The World Genetic Research Laboratory is getting support from several pharmaceutical companies and certain countries. The competition is intense as to who will be the first to make the breakthrough. They want to come up with cure for many such disorders and increase health and longevity for humanity. This laboratory is the best in the world with vast advanced facilities. People come from all over the world. They do charge for the treatments."

Chapter 12

The Gender

Don and John were enjoying the free time at the island. Nothing to do, no internet, no cell phones. The wives were in the treatment areas. So they used the time to continue probing their friends on further activities of the World Genetic Research Laboratory. This time, they talked about gender selection of newborn babies.

"Is that a real possibility that you can choose the gender, boy or girl, for your child?"

"Yes, but it involves certain special techniques that can be done only in an advanced laboratory like here."

"Tell us more about the gender determination of the child."

"The chromosomes determine the sex of the child. Male sex chromosome is XY, and female is XX. Normal cells have one of these two combinations in the form of a double helix. However, the double helix of the cells split to single helix when creating the germ cells. Hence, the sperm or ova has only one of these chromosomes. So the male sperm could be carrying either X or Y chromosome in it, whereas the female ova will be carrying X and X chromosome in it. When they unite at the time of fertilization, the double helix forms again as XY (male) or XX (female). Hence, the sex is finally determined out of the male sperm or man and not female egg or the woman."

"Is there a scientific reason for connection between father and son?"

"The DNA pattern of the father is passed on to the son in the Y chromosome and will be passed on the same way to his son and subsequent generation of sons and sons. Whereas the DNA pattern of the father and the daughter have X chromosome, but further generation of children will have her husband's chromosomes, either X or Y. Thus, the grandchildren born out of a daughter are no longer identical to the original grandfather. So it is a scientific theory that a man can have his identical Y chromosome passed on to generations of sons and their sons, but his chromosomal lineage ends when a daughter is born."

"We do not have personal preference between a boy or a girl."

"But that is not the case in many parts of the world. Gender of the unborn is a major issue in many parts of the world with preference being given to have male child over females even though it is well known that girls are more affectionate and caring of the parents than the boys. Some of this thinking has to do with the societal habits and cultures, but some of it may have a genetic background."

"But it does not appear to be an issue in the USA."

"Not true. Women did not have property rights or voting rights until one hundred years ago. Women did not have voting rights until recently even in the civilized Western world. She had no voice in politics or government and was not expected to go to work outside of their own farm or estate. Her job is to cook for the family, take care of the children, and do other household chores. Men go to work, earn a living, control finances, and make all major decisions. Women must stay indoor, take care of the house and children, and should not go out alone. Even today, women do not get paid equal for equal work, and they have to fight for their rights all the time."

"What is the history on this?"

"Kingdoms required a male heir to pass on the throne to the next generation. The head of state has to be a man. If a queen is the head of state, it is likely that she will not be present in the battlefield to provide leadership and motivation to the soldiers directly in the war field. Powerful ministers or captains of the military will make major policy decisions. Worse still would be the influence of her husband, who may end up transferring the dynasty to a totally different family. People always prefer a ruthless and strong man to be the head of state instead of a weak and soft lady. Foreign or enemy countries invade the nation or announce war when they hear that a lady is leading a nation. Wars can mean loss of wealth and slavery for the defeated one. It has been recorded in the history that certain kingdoms have kept the birth of girls as secret or announced them to be male and raised them as male princes just for this reason."

"How is it in India? We heard they conduct female infanticide there."

"In India, the matter can be even worse. Girls have to be married off at the right age as virgins and with no blemishes or bad marks. A hefty dowry has to be paid to get her married to the right male. If a man has three or more girls, he will go bankrupt to get all three married. It is a huge burden, and they blame the girl from the day she is born. The girl is cursed and neglected and is denied of good education, food, or amenities. Boys are preferentially treated and nurtured. Efforts are made to find the sex of the unborn child using ultrasound technique even though the government bans this practice. If it is a female fetus, they make all efforts to get it aborted. Female infanticide is common. Once the girl is married off, she is considered to be a member of her husband's family, severing all connections to her birth family. So if a man dies without a son, all his property and assets end up with the in-laws."

"What about Islamic countries?"

"Things are much worse in the Islamic countries. Women have absolutely no rights or value. The woman must stay as a slave. She cannot drive a car, cannot go out alone, and cannot work independently. Male children are preferred over female children. In these societies, the culture is male-dominated. Men dictate rules and regulations. Properties and wealth are transferred through male. Many civil rights are denied for female, who are considered to be slaves and sex objects only. Men can legally marry four women at same time, but women have to put up with the one who marries her irrespective of his age or health. Women do not get proper education so that they will remain as dependents of menfolk."

"Can you tell us about any patient who had the gender selection done in your place?"

"Yes. I recall the story of an Indian client by the name of Parasuram. Parasuram, who goes only by his first name, is a very wealthy industrialist in the city of Mumbai. But his mother cursed him every other day, saying, 'You will not go to heaven but will rot in the hell.'

He asked, 'Why?'

'Because when you die, there will be no son of yours to light the pyre to cremate your body. It will have to be done by some other man.'

'What is your problem?'

'That wife of yours is a cursed woman. She has given you four daughters but not a son. Only son of my son can give me salvation and give you salvation.'

'That is our fate. God has decided it that way. What are we supposed to do?'

'I don't know what you will do—marry another woman, take serious penance and prayers, or consult a specialist fertility doctor.'

"He is one frustrated man even though he has everything going good in his life. He is happily married to Jyothi. A beautiful and sincere wife, huge wealth and successful company in the IT field, big house in Juhu Beach, and envy of his classmates. But nothing is giving him comfort, since he has four daughters, each one and a half year apart, but no sons. His wife is depressed and even more worried since she is getting older. They have prayed to the God of procreation, tried different techniques and timings in their sexual intercourse, followed different diets and medications. Each time they prayed for a son, and each time they were disappointed. They are very conservative and religious, traditional in their thoughts that daughters have to be married off to a different family with a huge dowry, and their wealth will end up in another's family. Now they are willing to spend the money to have a son. They approached the World Fertility and Genetic Clinic in Mumbai for help. They had heard from word-of-mouth sources that the clinic could arrange the gender of a newborn child using their own genes and chromosomes.

THE CLINIC

"The World Fertility and Genetic Clinic promised to help the situation by separating the chromosomes and fertilizing the X with Y in the test tube and then implanting the zygote back into the uterus of Jyothi by way of in-vitro fertilization. It is illegal, but for the desperate ones, it is worth the money compared to the cost and aggravation of raising multiple girls versus making upfront one-time payment to have a male child of their own. High-level secrecy and privacy is needed, and cost is high. So Parasuram and his wife elected to seek consultation and treatment at the World Fertility and Genetic Clinic.

"The clinic agreed to make the appropriate arrangements. Both the male sperms and female ova were collected, deep-frozen, and sent to the World Genetic Research Laboratory. Here the X and Y chromosomes are separated, in-vitro fertilization was done using the Y chromosome, and the zygote was sent back to the local clinic. The local clinic implanted the zygote into the mother's uterus, allowing the male child to grow as a normal. Alternately, Parasuram and wife Jyothi were given the choice of spending a few days at the island with all modern facilities and hospital."

Jyothi did some reading and found some interesting observation on animals. In the case of turtles, alligators, and crocodiles, the temperature at the time of incubation of eggs determines sex and not the chromosomes. In turtles, lower temperature of seventy-eight to eighty-two degrees Fahrenheit makes all males. Temperatures above eighty-six degrees Fahrenheit make them all females. For alligators, warmer temperature of ninety-one degrees Fahrenheit makes them all males, and cooler temperature of eighty-four to eighty-eight degrees Fahrenheit makes them all female. It would be nice to have this feature available for humans!

"What is the history in this field of genetics?"

"It was an Augustinian monk by the name Gregor Mendel in 1865 who first proposed that traits are determined by genes. Until then, it was believed that God or supernatural forces determined traits. Mendel made his experiments on plants, creating hybrids. He noticed that genes were in pairs and postulated that sex cells had only one gene. He published his findings as 'experiments in plant hybridization' and sent copies to prominent scientists in different countries. However, it was discounted and turned down until 1900 when three European scientists confirmed his theories independently."

"What is the difference between regular cell division and sex cell division?"

"Normal cell duplication is done through a process called mitosis. All the cells have chromosomes, but they are in double. When the cell divides, it divides into two equal but smaller cells. The chromosomes duplicate, separate to two sides, and finally the cell cytoplasm and cell membrane also divide. However, during reproduction, a different process called meiosis occurs. Here the chromosomes unravel, and each germinal cell carries only one set of the chromosome in those germinal cells either in the sperm or in the ovum. After the fertilization, when these two unite, then the double chromosome is restored to create the new fetus. Afterward, it grows by mitosis again."

Finally, Parasuram and Jyothi had their own male child. The genetic laboratory was able to separate out the sperms with Y chromosome and had them mate with the egg. Now he will be able to go to heaven when he dies, since his own son will be able to light the pyre.

Chapter 13

The Parent

John asked his friend, "Tell us how your center is involved in DNA analysis in determining parenthood."

"Sure. Have you seen this billboard that blares the advertisement, 'Do you know who your parents are? Do you want to know your ancestry? Do you know where your cousins are? We can help you. Please contact the World Fertility and Genetic Clinic'?"

"Tell us some stories that you know of."

"Mr. Bill Chancy was a very famous television personality. He had acted on several TV serials and comedy shows. Some of them were named after him and were very popular among viewers. Like many of the handsome men of popularity, he did have some affairs, which he kept secret. Some of his associates knew about this weakness, but they kept the distance. One of his mistresses got pregnant. He persuaded her to get it aborted and paid her well. However, she wanted to have the child. Then he threatened her with violence and abandonment. She decided to move away from him, left town, and settled in another state. She raised her female child as a single mother.

"When the daughter reached the age of eighteen, she told her that Bill Chancy was her biological father. The daughter decided to seek justice from Bill Chancy and approached him for recognition that she is his daughter. Initially, all she wanted was a father's love and support. However, when Mr. Chancy refused to meet her and refused to talk to her, the reaction turned into one of vengeance. So she initiated legal action, requesting paternity determination and claiming inheritance share of his assets. The lawyers moved motion to dismiss the case as without merit. However, the daughter produced evidences of prior relationship between Chancy and her mother with witnesses of her mother, her old acquaintances, and old photographs. Finally, the court ordered a paternity determination test, which indeed proved that Mr. Chancy was her biological father. Mr. Chancy was not obligated to give any money despite this proof of paternity. He still had the right to allocate his assets, but he lost considerable fame and reputation."

"Why is our society currently challenging the parenthood more often than in the past?"

"It could be for reasons of legality, peace of mind, immigration, inheritance, and question of infidelity. Years ago, this was rarely a question. Loyalty, honesty, and morality were expected norms. Freedom was limited, and family was close-knit. Progress in science, changes in social structure, communication, transportation, and advancements in legal understandings have changed the world but have also brought in unforeseen issues. People sometimes have to ask, 'Who am I? Are you my real father or my real mother? Are you my real child? How can I get a share of your wealth and popularity?' Advent of social media such as Facebook, Google searches, Twitter, and LinkedIn have opened up far-reaching avenues for people to make contacts and discover lost family members."

"Has technology changed the behavior of people?"

"Artificial insemination is now accepted as a method of becoming pregnant. The question can be raised as to whose sperms were used in this process. Sometimes the husband is infertile, and the sperm is obtained from a sperm bank, which will keep the details anonymous, but the actual donor can be traced through the records, and the DNA analysis can verify that. The husband and wife may be keeping this as a secret, and the child is made to believe that they are the parents. As the child grows up, due to emotional outbursts or leaks or obvious physical appearances, the child realizes that the biological parent is different. In certain instances, the donor of the sperm is legally allowed to track down his progeny for the sake of information and love."

THE CLINIC

"Can there be lawsuits against the clinic?"

"Mistakes can happen in the fertility clinic when the sperms are mixed up with the egg, particularly in cases of in-vitro fertilization. More and more women are freezing their eggs for becoming pregnant at a convenient time in their life. Mistakes can happen in the genetic laboratory where mix-ups of both egg and sperm can happen, resulting in carrying someone else's progeny, all the while thinking it is one's own child. Some women need surrogate mothers, since they cannot carry the pregnancy by themselves. The egg and sperm can be from the husband and wife, but another woman carries the pregnancy to full term. Does she have any rights to the child? It is expected that she will have no claims to the child as agreed by contract before renting her uterus. However, it so happens that on occasions, the woman gets emotional with breast milk and other hormone changes and refuses to give up the child."

"Tell us more stories on determining parenthood by DNA analysis."

"This story relates to immigration and naturalization. The father was a White American and a Vietnam veteran. He spent nearly five years in the field. During this time, he met and married a Vietnamese lady and promised to bring her to United States up on his return from duty. They had a son legally from this wedlock. During the panic at the end of the war and the rush to have the soldiers returned to mainland, there was utter chaos and confusion. The soldier had to come back to the US alone. After a few months, he conveniently forgot about her and the child. The mother suffered painful experiences in the hands of the Vietnam soldiers, and she died. But she left all records and photos of her married life with the soldier and birth of the son, along with marriage certificate and birth certificate before she died. The son was a destitute and orphan in Vietnam and wanted to contact the legal biological father.

"After a long search, the son was able to locate the father and make contact with him. The soldier in the USA agreed that a son was born in Vietnam, but he had not seen him for the past eighteen years and wanted to verify if this person is legitimate or if he is a fake person. So they resorted to DNA paternity test and found that he was indeed his son. With all sorts of the documents, DNA analysis results, and sponsoring documents from the father, the son was able to become a US citizen. They reunited and started a new life together after eighteen years.

"Here is a claim for inheritance—Mr. Tim Jones was a multi-millionaire, who made his money on waste management. He was a self-made man and had married and divorced three times in his life. He died alone and left a will. It stated that the estate was to be divided among his children from his marriages. It dictated that children born to his ex-wives out of other men were not eligible for the inheritance. His first wife had remarried and had a child out of Tim Jones and another child from her second marriage. The second wife had previous marriage and a child before he met her. After marriage to Tim Jones, she delivered another child. The third wife had two children out of Tim Jones, but there was a rumor that the second child was from his cousin. Truth had never been established since he was going to divorce her anyway, knowing her misbehavior. So there were six children competing to get his estate, but it appears only three were eligible. The fourth child's father may be Tim Jones, but rumor is otherwise. It was stipulated that everyone take DNA analysis to prove paternity with Tim Joes, whose DNA sample and blood sample were specifically preserved for this purpose. As expected, the three legitimate children qualified for the inheritance. The fourth child's paternity was not Tim Jones. The real father's name remains undisclosed.

"Another one is looking for recognition and fame—Sam Singer was a famous actor, having acted main roles in three Oscar-winning movies. He was the personification of male macho and was loved by male and female admirers all over the world. He had mistresses galore even though he was married to movie actress Grace Thomas at one time. It was rumored that he had fathered at least five children but with no official records. Two of them, one girl and one boy, had made claims in the press that they are offspring of Sam Singer. Sam had denied of such children, but the children wanted recognition that Sam is their father. They were not after his money or estate. They just wanted the recognition as son and daughter of Sam. It would give them an edge in their own life in the acting world. They obtained a court order to get DNA verification of paternity after proving the relationship of their mothers with Sam with circumstantial evidence and photographs.

"Then there was this case based on desire for revenge—Chris Meter was seething with anger about his father. He knew from childhood that Mr. Gore cheated his mother after promising her a married life, love, and wealth. After sleeping with her for months, always postponing the wedding under one pretext or another, he abandoned her after knowing that she was carrying his baby. She begged and cried and was willing to do anything to please him to have legitimacy of their child. Mr. Gore became defensive and rude and kicked her out.

She went back to her poor life and instilled revenge and anger on Chris. She told him several times about the way Mr. Gore had cheated her and mistreated her. He was to take revenge on his father when he grew up. After considering various options, he decided it would be the best choice to make it known to the public and social media about his father—and claim his inheritance. He went after Mr. Gore, who had gotten older by this time, and had a court-ordered DNA analysis that confirmed his paternity. He wanted to punish Mr. Gore more than anything else. Under remorse and shame, Mr. Gore finally accepted Chris as his son and gave him some of his assets as inheritance.

"Some people just want to know the truth for personal information—Alicia just wanted to know who her biological mother and her surrogate mother were. The Vance family adopted her when she became an orphan at the age of three. She barely had any memory of her real mother who died in an automobile accident. When she became an adolescent, she came to know that she was an adopted child. She was thankful for the Vance family for having saved her life. She was curious to find out about her biological mother. Research and enquiries revealed that her real mother's name was Jenny. But Jenny could not have pregnancy of her own due to uterine and cervical problems. She had the ovaries that could produce eggs as normal. However, the uterus could not hold the pregnant fetus, so she had in-vitro fertilization of her egg with her husband Tony's sperms. Then the fertilized zygote was implanted inside the womb of her mother's sister, Mary.

"Mary carried the pregnancy to full term and delivered Alicia. By contractual agreement, Mary would not have any rights further on Alicia at any time. Jenny was happy to have her baby truly fertilized egg of herself and her husband, Tony. They were very happy and moved out of town to a different state and started a new life.

"When Jenny and her husband died in the automobile accident, Alicia became an orphan, and Mary wanted to have her. However, due to the quirks of law, she was unqualified to adopt her because of her financial status and past criminal records. The Vance family stepped in. Now Alicia wanted to reconnect with her real mother, Jenny, and her surrogate mother, Mary, out of curiosity. She just wanted to know the truths behind her life. She has been happy with the Vance family and will continue to stay with them. She is also thankful to have met Mary, who is her real aunt and her surrogate mother. Now they are all one big family."

"How does your clinic help in these situations?"

"For a fee, the World Fertility and Genetic Clinic helps the clients in determining parenthood for many individuals. The laboratory will conduct the genetic analysis, and DWS will provide necessary investigations and circumstantial proofs to make the case. It is just a matter of paying the fee for the service."

When there is a claim of fatherhood by a child, it is legally acceptable for the father to test that child for determining paternity without knowledge or permission from the mother. It is a proof to deny child support or even alimony. On the other hand, reverse paternity determination is possible when the father is not available for testing. It uses STR alleles in the mother and child, comparing with brothers or sisters of the alleged father. It is also legal for a father to test the DNA of his child without knowledge or permission from the child or mother to ensure that he is indeed the father. However, such secretive testing may not be permissible in the court of law.

"We heard of companies that will find your roots."

"Ancestry tracing, also known as genetic genealogy, is a well-known process, and there are many commercial companies undertaking this business. Many millions of people have taken the gene tests in the hopes of finding their ancestors and families and to know their roots. They involve testing the DNA and single base pair changes also known as single-nucleotide polymorphisms (SNP). SNPs can be unique to an individual or to a certain groups or clans. While it helps many people, it may also bring out unsuspected surprises such as undisclosed adoptions and infidelity in the family."

"How often is paternity questioned in the USA?"

"It is estimated that 1 to 5 percent of children in the USA are fathered by someone else other than the father listed in their birth certificate. The most famous case was that of past President Thomas Jefferson. In 1802, he was accused of fathering a son by one his slaves, Sally Hemings. DNA analysis of the son, Easton, was found to match the Y chromosome lineage of the Jefferson family.

"Here is another true story—after a decades-long search, Peter Shatner identified his biological father. Shatner was born on December 9, 1956, and then given up for adoption in New York by Canadian actress Kathy Burt, who is also now dead. His birth certificate reads 'Male McNeil,' reflecting the last name of Leonard McNeil—a man his biological mother was dating. In 1984, his biological mother told Shatner that his birth father was either William Shatner or a man she could only remember as Chick. She could not be sure.

"In 2009, Shatner sought answers by adding his DNA to Ancestry.com and looking for genetic matches through William Shatner's relatives. That is how, eleven years later, he found his connection to Chick's children. Chick's daughter agreed to take a DNA test. 'The test came back positive that she was my half sibling,' Shatner, sixty-three, said. Chick was a nickname. He was Benjamin Freedman, a Canadian citizen who died in 2001. It is upsetting, Shatner admitted, that he will never meet his birth father. 'I will never have the opportunity to sit and talk to him.'

"Charles McNeil, Shatner's half brother through his birth mother, confirmed that story. 'My mother had no reason to lie,'

McNeil said in 2015. 'If anything, she was ashamed of it, so she kept it very private. She could have tried to make money off her story but never did even when times were tough.' 'I found what I was looking for,' Shatner said. 'I finally know where I come from.'"

John and Don came to learn some other facts about ancestry tracing. A child inherits mitochondria from the mother and, thus, has more genetic identity to the mother than the father. Genes responsible for intelligence is in the X chromosome. Thus, the mother has higher chance of providing this trait than the father to the children. In childbearing and child raising, the mother is more involved than the father. The child feels more attachment and affinity to the mother than the father.

It is possible to have a twin born with two separate biological fathers if the mother had sex during the same cycle with two different men, leading to fertilization of two eggs with two separate sperms. It is not common but it is possible. DNA analysis will help clarify biological fathers.

DNA testing for paternity using Y chromosome—Y chromosome passes from the father to the son only. The father's identity can be determined even while the baby is in uterus by doing amniocentesis or chorionic villus sample or from the blood of the mother.

Mitochondrial DNA for maternal lineage—mitochondrial genome is good for maternity but not good for paternity.

Autosomal DNA—this testing is useful for both sides.

DNA can be determined from saliva, blood, urine, semen, hair, or bones.

Chapter 14

The Cloned

"Tell us something about your experiments on cloning."

"Yes, it is one of the major projects here. The secret is that we are trying it on humans unlike anywhere else in this planet."

"Wow. Who are the people wanting it done?"

"There are many rich and egoistic people who feel that they are the best and even their natural-born children cannot replace them. So they want themselves cloned."

"Tell us some examples, if it is okay."

"We are not allowed to disclose names, and privacy is guaranteed. But I can mention that a certain past president of the USA and a certain billionaire from China have had their initial work done here for that purpose."

"What is the background on this type of work?"

"Animals have been cloned in the past. Still, there are a number of ongoing projects in various stages on animal experiments. But the most sought after and the most expensive and most dangerous one is cloning of humans. It is considered illegal and immoral in all countries. But it is appealing and imaginative for highly intelligent and highly successful people to have their own body reproduced and take over their role after their current body has become old and weak. World Genetic Research Laboratory is the one and only sophisticated and well-equipped place in the world where genius scientists work on this type of research."

"What is special about cloned babies?"

"Children by the conventional pregnancy are going to be a mixture of man and his woman. Some features of the offspring will be the same, but some features will be different. Cloned babies will be exactly identical to the parenting person. This is more appealing to men than women."

"Are there any possibility of cloned humans at all?"

"Currently the only cloned babies that we know of are identical twins, where a single fertilized zygote splits into two, giving rise to two exactly identical babies. Some identical twins may not have identical DNA due to mutations in early development. Cloning of humans appears to be an impossible task at this time."

"But natural-born babies can also be as good as their father, is it not?"

"I shall tell you a story. A lady approached Bernard Shaw after a speech by him. She was very impressed by his intelligence. She considered herself to be the most beautiful. She proposed to Bernard Shaw to marry her. He asked her the reason for her proposal, since they had just met casually. She said that with her beauty and his intelligence, they could have a child, combining those two features, that will be most intelligent and most beautiful. So Bernard Shaw asked her what is the guarantee that it won't be the other way around—child with his beauty and her intelligence. She felt ashamed and left the scene."

"What is involved in cloning?"

"Cloning is a process of reproducing a genetically identical cell, organ, or the whole body by replication instead of the process of meiosis, where a male and female germ cells are combined to create a new life. It is well known that cells can multiply spontaneously. Unicellular organisms like the bacteria, fungi, and amoeba duplicate themselves. Cloning also happens in the plant kingdom, where by the exact same plant is reproduced unlike the humans."

"So what is involved in the process?"

"Even though it sounds simple, cloning is a complicated process. A cloned body is created by asexual method, but it still requires the DNA, an unfertilized egg, and a biotechnology lab to create a zygote, blast it off the egg components, then implant the DNA zygote in a live uterus and grow it to delivery."

"When was the first cloned animal created?"

"On July 5, 1996, Dolly the sheep became the first successfully cloned mammal at Roslyn Institute in Scotland. It was first code-named as 6LL3 but was renamed after the singer Dolly Parton, since the cells were taken from the udder of a six-year-old host. Dolly was subsequently mated with a male sheep called David and gave birth to four calves. Dolly developed arthritis and died of lung problems in 2003 by the age of six."

"Is there any commercial work being done on this method?"

"Not exactly by cloning but by indirect methods. Even though cloning of humans is prohibited and discouraged from social, ethical, and moral points of view, it is getting a certain level of acceptance. Skin cells can now be coaxed to become stem cells and then other organs. This can benefit transplantation of organs. Novartis sells laboratory-grown skin grafts cultured from a small amount of skin procured from prepuce of newborn males, denatured against any allergens. These grafts can cover raw surfaces and heal and function similar to freshly procured autogenous grafts taken from one's own body."

"We have watched certain science-fiction movies on this topic."

"Yes. There are fiction stories where famous people and autocrats tried to clone themselves, lending to imagination and mystery. Science-fiction movies are made where cloned bodies are used as sources of organs for transplantation to the parent when needed. The cloned body is sacrificed if necessary once the organ is procured. More such cloned bodies can be created as the need arises. Very wealthy people for their own benefit fund the World Genetic Research Laboratory."

"What are some problems in evaluating the progress of a cloned baby?"

"The cloned baby has to be tested to make sure it is identical to the parent, and then it has to be allowed to grow to adulthood. The cloned person has to be monitored for lifelong period. How to keep the cloned baby safe, how to nurture it, how to educate it, and how to give it emotional and social support? Is it better for the baby to live with parents, or is it better off in the custody of the laboratory? There are some unknown and unchartered territories to be explored."

"Can a man clone himself?"

"For a man to clone himself, he still needs a woman with a healthy uterus to carry the cloned child through the term of pregnancy. But for a woman, she can carry her own cloned baby if she is healthy. If not, she will need a surrogate woman to carry her child through pregnancy."

"What do you do with the woman who carried the baby through pregnancy?"

"It is open for question. Should she be paid for the services, never to return for any claims thereafter? Should she be killed so that she never shows up anywhere? What type of person should be selected for this job? How about an African slave? Or how about an abducted human-trafficked destitute? She is fed and given shelter inside the laboratory, held captive as a prisoner. Or should it be a healthy surrogate woman from the clinic for money with written contractual agreement?"

"Did they clone any other animals?"

"Since history was made when Dolly was born in 1996, there have been a few other animals cloned. Most noteworthy cloning was two months ago, done in San Diego Zoo in the division of frozen zoo under San Diego Zoo Global research, when a rare near-extinct horse was cloned. The baby colt, which is a Przewalski's horse, is called Kurt, named after a genetic scientist. There are only two thousand of such horses alive worldwide now. The special feature is that it was cloned from the skin cells taken from a stallion forty years ago in 1980 and deep-frozen at minus 320 degrees. Similar cells from 1,100 species have been saved in the frozen zoo there. The scientists revived the skin cells and fused them with unfertilized egg from a domestic horse after removing the nucleus from the egg. Thus, the egg was holding mostly only the colt's DNA, carrying all the genetic material from the original stallion. Then the team transplanted the egg back inside the uterus of the domestic horse, which in effect became the surrogate mother."

"So the environmentalists must be interested in this type of resurrection."

"In the year 2018, an organization by the name of Revive and Restore received the first-ever permit to research cloning of endangered species. They have successfully cloned black-footed ferret in the San Diego zoo. These ferrets almost vanished from the face of earth in 1980. Knowing this at that time, geneticist Dr. Ryder had deep-frozen the skin segments of the last dead ferret. Now, nearly forty years later, the skin cells were revived, cloned, and the new embryo was implanted into a domestic ferret as a surrogate. The baby ferret is noted to have all the features of the old black-footed ferret and was called Elizabeth Ann. Subsequently more of the ferrets have been cloned. The new babies are being carefully watched and seen if they can have naturally born babies of their own. Then the remedy for endangered species will be conclusively set."

"Have they cloned animals for profit motive?"

"One of the millionaire members of the DWS is interested in cloning racehorses from previous wins. This winner horse has fetched already $10 million in prize money. Soon it will become old. So why not have his clone prepared now? Another one wants to clone his pet dog, and third one wants to clone special breed of cows that give double the amount of milk."

"What do they generally do with the cloned body?"

"One person's objective is to kill the cloned person to take out organs for self-transplantation when in need. Another person will just remove the organ when in need without killing the whole cloned body. Lastly, some allow the old person to die and replace their life with the new young cloned offspring. The only place that will undertake these jobs is the World Genetic Research Laboratory."

"Are there any prehistoric mythology stories related to this topic?"

"Egyptian God Osiris had his body resurrected and recomposed after having been torn into multiple pieces and thrown into the river Nile. Greek mythology creature Hydra had multiple heads and could regenerate any of its head after being cut off. Finally, Hercules killed it by cutting the heads and burning the stumps immediately.

Prometheus was chained to a mountain where an eagle would eat his entrails, which he would regenerate the same day. This was given to him as a punishment for revealing the secret of fire to humans.

"Aristotle in 384 to 322 BC recorded that lizards could regenerate tails that were cut off. The Hindu epic story of Ramayana describes the demon god Ravana having ten heads. If any one of the heads were severed, he would regenerate the same immediately. Finally, Rama, the supreme god reincarnated as a king, cut off all ten heads simultaneously with a single special arrow. Hindus also believe in reincarnations. The Lord is supposed to have taken ten incarnations to save the world from destruction and disasters."

Chapter 15

The Stem Cell

"Do you perform stem cell work here?" asked Don.

"Yes, it is part of the work we do here. It is a cutting-edge technology that is still evolving and could turn out to be a multimillion-dollar business."

"What are stem cells for our understanding?"

"Stem cells are special kind of cells that have unique capacity to renew themselves or give rise to special type of new cells. The cell remains uncommitted until it receives a signal. Stem cells are body's raw material. From stem cells, all other types of cells with specialized function can be generated."

"Are there different types of stem cells?"

"There are three types of stem cells known to exist—they are embryonic stem cells, adult stem cells, and induced pluripotent cells."

"How are they different?"

"Embryonic stem cells (ESC) are isolated from the gonadal ridge of five- to ten-week fetus. They can turn into any type of cell. Adult stem cells are of value to maintain, renew, or repair tissues in disease."

"What about the third type of stem cells?"

"It is the induced pluripotent stem cell (iPSC). It is cultured out of skin cells after modifying their genes and can be used to grow any type of body tissue in a laboratory. This holds high future use."

"How are the adult stem cells collected?"

"Adult stem cells can be collected from umbilical cord blood of newborns. They can also be collected from blood of adults after giving them a course of special medicine and the sediments are filtered out."

"How do stem cells help in treating diseases?"

"Stem cell therapy is used to treat many medical conditions such as spinal cord injury, muscular dystrophy, heart diseases, brain damage, burns, cancer conditions, and blood disorders. Regeneration of diseased or degenerated body parts or vital organs has been a dream for a long time."

"What are other future uses of stem cells?"

"Stem cells can be used in the business of organ transplantation. Any of the different organs can be grown in the laboratory for such use."

"You mean to say that you can artificially grow any organ such as heart, lung, or brain in the petri dish in your lab?"

"Yes, it can be done. That is how the first cell of the zygote created various organs in the first place. If we can coax the embryonic stem cell to repeat the task, it can grow organs in the lab."

"No kidding. Are you for real?"

"You are right in a way. At present, we are only making cells of different organs and not the whole organ. We are commercially successful in making skin sheets."

"If you made only cells of different organs instead of the whole organs, how can you use them?"

"Stem cells can also be used to repair a damaged organ instead of replacing the entire organ. Thus, one can regrow dead cells in the heart following a heart attack or regrow brain cells following a stroke. The stem cells that are trained to become a specific organ tissue are injected into the diseased organ, thus making it healthy again. Thus, the organ transplantation can be reduced, and long-term illness can be avoided. This way, we can regenerate a diseased heart, lung, or brain."

"Is there any other option to use stem cells in organ transplantation?"

"Another option we try is to insert stem cells inside the denatured matrix of a whole organ."

"Explain this second option to us."

"For example, you need a kidney transplant but no suitable matched kidney is available. Now you take any kidney, denature it, and de-immunize the cells, and so it has only the structure. Now you insert stem cells into it and make it active again. This reactivated kidney with stem cells is transplanted to the patient."

"That is amazing technology."

John intervened to change the conversation.

"They call certain cancer treatments as stem cell therapy back home. What is involved here?"

"Bone marrow has stem cells. It is extracted out and it is infused back into cancer patients after giving them high-dose chemotherapy. They are called bone marrow transplants or stem cell therapy."

"What about the advertisements on stem cell therapy in ordinary commercial clinics? Are they any good?"

"It is not truly stem cell therapy. It is use of platelet-rich plasma. Blood drawn from a person is centrifuged, and the sediment that is rich in platelets and other components is collected. It is injected into areas of muscle damage or fractures for faster healing and is also called stem cell therapy in the commercial world."

"Are gene therapy the same as stem cell therapy?"

"They are different, but gene therapy and stem cell therapy intermingle in developing treatment for many congenital disorders. They hold similar future."

"These treatments must be expensive."

"Profit margins are mind-boggling. Already certain treatments are available in the market. They cost anywhere from $1 to 2 million for one patient."

"How has your center benefited?"

"World Genetic Research Laboratory is interested in conducting this work, which will not be permitted in the civilized world. Wealthy individuals and corporations that cross the boundaries of nations need it and fund it."

"What other new developments are happening in this field?"

"At Kyoto University in Japan, research is being done to make artificial blood out of stem cells. Platelets out of stem cells are being used to treat aplastic anemia."

"Do you recall any patient who had such advanced therapy?"

"This is true story of a seven-year-old male child in Syria, who developed epidermolysis bullosa. It is a rare lethal condition where the entire skin becomes fragile, breaks up, develops bullae, and then ruptures, losing over 80 percent of surface skin in a short time and resulting in death. Doctors were able to remove one small patch of healthy skin, send it to a special laboratory in Italy to isolate stem cells out of it, and then manufacture new skin sheets out of it. The new skin made in the laboratory was then placed on the body surface of the child. The dying child survived and is now healthy otherwise. This is an example of international collaboration—the child is Syrian, doctors were German, the laboratory is Italian, which was mentored by American—victory for humanity.

"A similar situation happens when there is over 40-percent body surface area involved in a burn victim. Mortality is very high in such cases. Stem cell therapy as well as artificial skin coverage can save many of these patients."

"Does the World Genetic Research Laboratory have its own secret sources of getting stem cells?"

"We are not allowed to talk about it. It would be a good deal to get a new fetus at five to ten weeks of pregnancy. One source is of course the abortion clinics across the world. Another source is humans kept captive in the World Genetic Research Laboratory. Women are impregnated with or without consent, and the baby is aborted or removed alive by surgery for the purpose of harvesting embryonic stem cells."

Chapter 16

The Sequencing

"So tell us how important the DNA is."

"DNA is life. DNA holds vast amount of information about cell function. DNA in all different animals works in the same fashion as in humans. It defines the very existence and behavior of every living organism."

"What is in the DNA?"

"It has four chemicals—adenine, guanine, thiamine, and cytosine. They are arranged in the same sequential pattern as a double helix of staircase."

"Is that what they call sequencing?"

"Sequencing is the study of the pattern of the genes, chromosomes, and chemicals inside the DNA."

"How many chromosomes and genes are there in human cells?"

"There are twenty-two pairs of autosomal chromosomes and one pair of sex chromosome with a total of twenty-three pairs. Inside there are three billion base pairs of DNA containing about 22,300 genes. Translating the genetic code is done with the help of RNA (ribonucleic acid). DNA provides a template for transcription. The RNA carries it as messenger RNA out of the nucleus to the cytoplasm of the cell to provide building plans to make proteins or polypeptides. Surprisingly, human genome sizes are smaller than many other animals, plants, and fish. There are 22,300 protein codes in the human genes."

"How easy is it to analyze this?"

"Let us imagine that someone is given a task to open a mystery number lock by finding the sequence and a combination of forty-six numbers that is held in a pair of twenty-three each. For most people, it will be impossible to open such a lock of mystery. Unlocking the mystery of an ordinary cell with forty-six chromosomes held in pair of twenty-three each is such a task. That is God's lock on life. Computerization, software development, big databases that can be shared, and international cooperation have helped to advance the human genome project."

"What is the practical use of such study?"

"With this type of study, we are able to find out which genes control what functions, understand basis for congenital disorders, understand causes of cancer, and develop drug therapies and gene therapies. This will help with early detection of various metabolic disorders even if the baby appears healthy. This will then enable early treatment, thus increasing higher chance for cure."

"Is it a marketable business?"

"Sequencing of human genome is a very big business. Company by the name Illumina started as a small firm ten years ago. It is now having a market capitation of $58 billion. It says that only 0.1 percent of humans had their genome sequenced. The cost of sequencing and the time requirement have come down with newer technologies. Previously it was done manually and took very many months to complete one genome. Now they can be done in days. It is expected that every single newborn child will have its genome sequenced in the future. DNA-based medications are being developed to treat cancers and certain metabolic disorders."

"What is the history on this type of work?"

"Human genome project was started in 1990 with the support of NIH and was completed in 2009. But there were three hundred gaps remaining as of 2020. Currently, seventy-nine gaps still remain. Work still continues on the genome sequencing. President Bill Clinton declared that genome sequence and associated research cannot be patented and wanted the information to be in public domain for further research by all. Still, private companies such as Celera were involved in private research for corporate gains."

THE CLINIC

"Can genes be patented?"

"According to a Supreme Court ruling, genes cannot be patented. It is just scientific information."

"What is your laboratory doing in this field?"

"One of the active projects of World Genetic Research Laboratory is sequencing of genomes. Wealthy people are willing to pay for it, to benefit their children, to identify treatable diseases early on, and to undertake appropriate therapy. They may even be able to completely cure them by instituting gene therapy inside the uterus before the baby is born."

"What are some gene-related anomalies in the newborn?"

"Gene-related congenital anomalies are well known. For example, Down syndrome is associated with one extra chromosome in 21 called as trisomy 21. Both males and females can have an extra X chromosome. Females with extra X chromosome are called trisomy X, who tend to be taller but with lower IQ. Males with extra X chromosome are called Klinefelter syndrome, and they tend to be taller and infertile. When there is only one X chromosome with no second chromosome, it is called monosomy X or Turner syndrome. Women with this syndrome are shorter and have no puberty resulting in infertility."

The World Genetic Research Laboratory can perform the sequencing studies and possibly correct the abnormal chromosomes, thus making these children normal again.

"What about cancer treatments?"

"Same thing goes for cancer treatments too. Some of these patients are considered to be having advanced disease with very little hope of recovery. With gene therapy, many of them can be controlled. A simple commonly used test in treating breast cancers is called HER2 (human epidermal growth factor receptor 2). It is a test measuring overexpression of the HER2 gene. Those who have the overexpression (HER2 positive) can be treated with a certain drug called trastuzumab (Herceptin), which is an antibody against HER2 protein. This test and treatment is done routinely for every breast cancer nowadays, but it was unknown even up to twenty years ago."

"Has it helped in other areas of health care?"

"Lots of resources are being allocated to control the COVID-19 infection. Sequencing of the coronavirus has led to the genetic makeup of the virus and creation of the mRNA technology vaccine by Pfizer and Moderna. The federal government has allocated $1.7 billion to sequence the coronavirus fully. There are thirty thousand genomes in the coronavirus. Decoding the genome helps to identify new mutations as they occur. It is this type of ongoing research on sequencing that enabled development of vaccines against COVID-19 within one year. They also had genomic information on the SARS virus, which had affected us a few years ago. In the past, the development of effective vaccine took several years of intense effort. The technology will be greatly useful to fight future pandemics, bacterial or viral in origin."

"How costly is it to do genomic sequencing?"

"Cost of sequencing the genes has come down significantly. Sequencing used to cost up to $150,000. Now it is down to $100. It is useful to test for risk for cancers and identify best drugs. Artificial intelligence is helping in this. However, as the virus mutates, constant analysis and data processing will be needed to detect the mutants early on. More important is for the governments to invest in education, research, and development. This budgeting gets hacked all the time due to politics and policies. The World Genetic Research Laboratory gets the job done without interruptions, and results benefit the entire humanity. Governments do support this venture covertly."

Chapter 17

The Editing

"We heard that you could create custom-made babies, what they call designer babies here. Is that true?"

"Yes, to a certain extent but not quite there yet. It is being tried seriously. We are not completely successful yet."

"How is it possible to do such a work?"

"In certain situations, it is easy to satisfy the client. For example, by choosing the sperm from a right type of male, the female can reasonably hope for the desired race, height, and intelligence."

"Tell us more difficult situations."

"Creating the desired gender is more involved, but we can do it. We have to separate out the sperms with Y chromosome and discard the ones with X chromosome if they want a male child and vice versa if they want a female child. Then that sperm is used for fertilization either in vivo or in vitro."

"What is even more difficult?"

"To change the genes or modify the genes of a baby that is already growing inside the womb to change the genes that are responsible for certain disorders or genetically transmitted conditions. But it is being tried with varying success."

"How about increasing longevity?"

"Yes, there are eight genes that have been identified so far that can increase longevity. We are working on animal models to increase life span of mice, pigs, and dogs. We think we can increase longevity of humans in the near future. At least by correcting the disorders by genetic technology, we can allow many people to live longer."

"Tell us some of your client's stories."

"Linda Turner became a very wealthy woman by marriage to Bob Turner. He made his millions in the mining fields and died prematurely from black lung disease. Now she has decided to become a mother at the age of forty without getting married to another man. She is a member of DWS and a regular user of the amenities offered. She bid for the sperms of a Nobel Prize winner in physics and wanted to have the World Genetic Research Laboratory edit it to have height and athletic abilities added to the brainpower of the potential father. Then she had the modified sperm inserted as artificial insemination. She preferred it this way instead of editing the embryo itself. She got pregnant and had the child of her specifications. Now we have to wait for the child to grow up and evaluate his achievements in life. Time will tell."

"How about another client."

"Victoria Gray, a Mississippi woman, was having sickle cell disease. She was effectively cured of it by having her stem cells removed, edited with CRISPR and reinfused with the treated cells. She would no longer carry the disease and would no longer pass it on to her children or grandchildren. But she had to pay over $1 million for the treatment. Is it worth it? I would say yes for sure. One can also rectify the mutation in the early-stage embryo of a sickle cell parent before birth."

"Is gene editing of embryos bad or illegal?"

"One of the major activities of the World Genetic Research Laboratory is to create gene-edited human embryos. Obviously, this is a banned procedure at this time in all countries and all facilities, since the outcome is unknown. The fear is that the gene-edited babies will have permanently altered genes in them, and they could transfer those new genes to their offspring. The change of events could be good for the human race, or it may be bad. The human race could be altered permanently and is somewhat scary."

"Are they realistic in this type of thinking?"

"Even though all the regulatory commissions and governments have condemned it, slowly they are beginning to recognize the need to relax these restrictions. Now they are of opinion that if there are no other options to have a child without diseases, or if a single gene modification alone will correct a disorder permanently, then it is allowable if the country agrees. Disorders such as muscular dystrophy, cystic fibrosis, beta thalassemia, and Tay-Sachs disease, which is a neurological disorder, fall in this category."

"What has changed by way of technology in this field to make it a possibility?"

"Even though it was known from 1975 that some sequence of DNA could be changed, recent discovery of CRISPR-Cas9 technology has made it more precise and cheaper. It stands for clustered regularly interspaced short palindromic repeats, and Cas9 is an enzyme that helps the process. With this method, a certain specific sequence of the DNA can be cut precisely and repaired, resulting in a new DNA sequence. When it is done at the extreme beginning of pregnancy to the immediately fertilized egg, the change is permanent to the newborn and to the subsequent generation of offspring."

"Is it possible for things to go wrong?"

"The technology is nascent and has many complications. Sometimes it cuts the DNA in unwanted places, and sometimes the repair is not done properly. The result is a mutation of the original, which is permanent and can be passed on as mutant for generations. There are many unknowns when one meddles with nature."

"Has anyone done this in real life so far?"

"It is possible to created gene-edited human babies. Using this technique, He Jiankui, a Chinese scientist, two years ago, claimed to have created designer babies. His goal was to have twin girls protected from HIV virus the parents had. There was an immediate condemnation and outburst all across the globe, since this could lead to immoral or illegal practices to create gene-edited designer babies. It shocked the civilized world, and he was imprisoned and fined for violating the rules. Chinese government arrested him and punished him with imprisonment and took away his license to practice in genetic field."

"He had good intentions. Don't you think that others will follow him for certain situations?"

"There are always rogue scientists who want to perform procedures for monetary gains or for personal achievements. There is great demand to have 'designer babies.' These are babies made to look or perform according to the desires of the mother. They want to have children with best athletic abilities, best scholastic abilities, or best looks. Whether a legal system allows it or not, those with money and power will always find a way. The World Genetic Research Laboratory fills that need. The line between therapy and personal enhancement is fuzzy and difficult to enforce. It is expected that many wealthy elites are covertly supporting the research on this field for personal gains."

"What is gene modification?"

"Gene modification is somewhat different from gene editing. Gene modification is selectively growing certain plants or animals in a preferential or intentional way so that the undesired slowly perishes and the desired ones grow. This is seen commonly in the agricultural field where the farmers prefer to grow cash crops instead of wild growths. Useful animals and domesticated ones are grown such as cows and horses over wildlife. The same can be said about ignoring girls over boys in certain societies. It is not a surprise if someone wants a White child over a Black one. It is a personal preference."

"Is it the same as eugenics?"

"Eugenics is still different, where the undesired ones are destroyed and selective reproduction of the chosen ones is encouraged to improve the society as a whole. Some people believe that they are superior to others, their clan is to be supported, and the underclass citizens can be sacrificed. History shows Adolf Hitler promoted this idea and was accepted by the Germans. Initially it was because of budget and financial issues. He promoted the idea that the mentally and physically disabled citizens in the state are burdens for the society as they take up a great deal of resources with no returns. So the state needed to support only those who are healthy and productive, and others can be ignored. Later on, this was expanded to Jews and homosexuals and criminals in the country. This was followed by the

Holocaust where hundreds and thousands of such people were killed. The leader was so convincing to the extent that many German scientists and military willingly participated in this protocol.

"Social and ethical problems are immense in a world with so much injustice, diversity, and discrimination. Race, religion, wealth, nationality, and gender, along with personal qualities, affect the life of a given individual and society as a whole.

"Currently all nations denounce, discourage, and prohibit human genome editing for the newborn because the social and ethical implications are unfathomable. How will the mutants look like and behave, especially when they can pass on the mutant status to their offspring? Will it increase diversity, will it help LGBTQ, or will it help minorities and women or shortchange them? When we alter Mother Nature, will it bring destruction of the world in a deceptive way?"

"Are there companies doing some type of gene editing already?"

"Crispr Therapeutics, Intellia Therapeutics, Editas Medicine, and Beam Therapeutics are gene-editing companies whose stocks have doubled within the past few months. They hope to treat inherited genetic disorders and cancers in new ways. The next generation on this is called base editing. Beam Therapeutics is involved in this. Base editing has potential to cure a condition called progeria, which prematurely ages and kills children. Median life span for these children is fourteen years now. It is due to one single defect in the gene. Experiments on mice show promising result in prolonging their life."

"Has there been drugs approved based on this type of work?"

"In the year 2017, FDA approved Luxterna for genetic defect that leads to blindness (Sparks/Roche Labs). Next, they approved Zolgensma for muscular dystrophy (AveXis/Novartis). Even though both of these are rare diseases, the one-time treatment was set for over $1 million per treatment as a chance of cure instead of prolonged therapies and disabilities."

"Who invented this type of technology?"

"Jennifer Doudna, a biochemist at Berkeley, California, received the Nobel Prize in 2020 for helping to invent the CRISPR-Cas9 technology. This is a technique bacteria have been using to fight off viruses for over a billion years. The bacteria are able to develop clustered repeated sequences that can recognize the viruses and discard them from its DNA."

"What are their goals?"

"Researchers have already worked on creating bigger mouse and muscular cattle. It is only a matter of time athletes want to have a bigger frame or stronger body with larger muscles similar to Hercules. Work is being done to gene-edit neurological disorders such as schizophrenia, bipolar disorder, and Alzheimer's disease. So why not request for a baby with higher intelligence or IQ to be more successful in this competitive world?

"Many more Einstein-like children can advance science to new frontiers. Harvard gene-editing pioneer George Church says, 'I don't see why eliminating a disability or giving a kid blue eyes and fair skin or adding 15 IQ points is going to be a threat to public health or morality of the world.' It should be the parents' choice and decision as any other reproductive rights. The government should stay out of this and let individual people decide what they want with their body and their children."

"How is this going to change the life of ordinary citizens?"

"Future fertility clinics will be able to help not only in getting pregnant but also with the baby. Your own inherited disorders and diseases should not be transmitted to the children as a genetic disorder. They should be corrected in the embryo stage itself. Moreover, you should be able to choose the type of baby you want, irrespective of your marital status.

"Loving your spouse has nothing to do with the kind of child you are going to have. Why leave it to nature with all the unpredictability for the newborn baby, from gender to health and intelligence to body stature? Certainly no one wants a child who is going to be blind or deaf or with mental disability. No one wants a dwarf or midget or one with mongolism. Extra premium price is acceptable for enhancements such as height, weight, IQ, skin color, hair color, and eye color. So-called diversity will be by choice and not left up to natural selection."

"Why do they consider gene editing as unethical?"

THE CLINIC

"Today we collectively say that it is unethical to do gene editing of human embryos. But there may come a time when it would be considered unethical *not* to perform gene editing of an embryo when it is clear that the baby will be born with certain congenital disabilities. It has taken millions of years for nature to weave together three billion base pairs to make the DNA of humans. Sometimes they are imperfect and with many diversities. Correcting one or two spots in that big chain may not affect human race after all. Gene therapy and CRISPR technology have opened up new avenues. It may look mysterious, promising, and creating hope for mankind, but it may also be fraught with new dangers. Only time will tell."

"Do you think the world will change from a gender point of view?"

"The future of the world is in the hands of women and not men. She has the reproductive organs to create a child, she has the breast milk to nourish the baby, she has the hormones to get through with pregnancy and lactation, she has the mindset and temperament to raise the baby, whereas all that men can offer is just one sperm. She can acquire that one sperm donated from any number of sources, from men of different backgrounds and from different time periods. It is her choice whether to go with standard natural sex with a married husband or with a sperm from man of her choice or one from a sperm bank. The sperm can be in cold storage for a number of years to be thawed. She can freeze her own eggs to be thawed for a future date when she is ready. She can have the baby genetically edited to her liking without any defects or disorders."

"Are you doing anything very unique in this laboratory?"

"The World Genetic Research Laboratory grows a special type of unisex babies. These are babies grown with no X chromosome or Y chromosome, along with the removal of all sex-related genes from the DNA. These children have no sex organs as they are born—they are unisex. They have neither female organs such as vagina, uterus, or ovaries nor development of breasts. Also, they do not have male organs such as scrotum, testes, or penis. The bottom end is just plain and smooth with an opening for the rectum for defecation and another one in front for urination.

"These are sexless babies with no hormones related to sexuality. As they grow, they become the workhorses for the society with no distractions, discriminations, or differences. They are all equal. They clone themselves to increase the workforce without needing conventional reproduction. The world will need many such soldiers who will just serve the society and government with no questions asked. Look at the ants or bees. Vast majority of them are just workers. One or two queens in a nest just to produce more new workers. We need a lot of good workers with total focus on work. There will be no such thing as sexual discrimination, sexual harassment, or Me Too movement. All are equal in this society. Reproduction is assigned to a specific group of mothers."

"Any stories from mythology relating to this type of science?"

"Greek mythology has a story of a man named Minotaur with a bull face and the rest of the body being human. He was the son of Minos the King and his wife, Pasiphae. Poseidon, the god of seas, had sent a white bull to Minos as a gift with instructions to butcher it. However, he kept the bull instead of sacrificing it. Hence, Poseidon cursed that Pasiphae, the queen, will fall in love with the bull. One day, the queen visited the bull, disguising herself as a white cow. The queen ended up conceiving and gave birth to Minotaur as half human and half bull. This was mythology but telling us how a gene editing went wrong."

Chapter 18

The Harvesting

"With your availability of cloned organs, do you send those organs to other countries or do you perform the transplantations here itself?"

"We do both, depending upon the request of the clients."

"So do you have full transplantation facilities here?"

"Of course. We have a first-class hospital attached to the World Genetic Research Laboratory. Your wives are here, and you have seen it firsthand. We have the best transplant surgeons and technicians right here."

"Organ procurement and organ sale must be a very lucrative business."

"Obviously it is. There is a huge demand for organs for transplantation all over the world. The biggest handicap in spite of all the progress in science and surgery is still lack of availability of suitable organs in a timely fashion. The World Genetic Research Laboratory with the help of Dark Web Site and an efficient communication system and transportation system can provide the organs at short notice to any hospital in the world. Alternatively, it can also have the patient transported to the island and have the surgery done there at short notice. Cost is high, but for those who need it, cost is not an issue. It is the result that matters."

"How successful is the organ transplantation?"

"Organ transplantation is an accepted treatment now. It was an unknown science one hundred years ago. Much scientific advancement has been made in this last century. Techniques in surgery have improved. Medications to suppress rejection were discovered. Better matching is done with advanced protocols. Hundreds of thousands of patients are living longer and healthier."

"What is the biggest logistic problem in this field?"

"But still, the biggest logistic problem is the availability of suitable organs for those waiting for the transplantation. There is a need for willing donors. Properly matching organs and timely availability and a ready transplant team are all of essence. Organ banks such as life link facilitate the process. There are many legalities to be fulfilled such as documentation of death or brain death, family consent, and lack of communicable diseases or cancers in the deceased."

"We have heard of stories when a kidney was removed without the patient's knowledge. Is it true?"

"There are many horror stories in places such as India, where kidneys have been removed without consent from patients or donated for a large cash payment. These organs are then transplanted to rich people such as the Arabic sheiks. Hospitals support the deals since it is a lucrative business."

"Do you have all the necessary setup to perform a transplantation procedure here in this island?"

"The World Genetic Research Laboratory has a full-fledged operating suite with all modern amenities and world-class transplant surgeons and operating crew stationed on-site in the island. Dr. Stanley Harold is a top-class transplant surgeon, and he works in coordination with Dr. Mark Steward, who is a great neurosurgeon in conducting various transplants that have not been done before. Whenever there is a suitable patient flown in, they can perform the operation and admit the patient for postoperative care and close monitoring until the patient is fully recovered."

"What are the sources for obtaining organs at your center?"

"Essentially the organs for transplantation come from one of the three sources at this facility. First, it can be a laboratory grown organ from an embryonic stem cell with pluripotent capacity, cultured and matured and ready to go. If necessary, such embryonic cells will be harvested out of newly conceived embryos after aborting these babies.

"Secondly, it can be harvested out of cloned body specially grown for the organ donation in times of need. Finally, it can also be harvested out of one of the captives held and nurtured in the island for this special purpose. They are usually typed and matched and kept in good health. An organ can be delivered to any hospital in the world for transplantation within twenty-four hours. Once the order is made and money is received, the organ will be shipped in cold storage box, alive and in good condition for immediate use. The cost would be high, but for the buyer, it is a lifesaver."

"Is that how you get transplantable organs at short notice?"

"The facility holds a large number of captives who are healthy individuals. They were unwanted by the society and had been written off as missing individuals. Every one of these captives is medically examined, tested, blood groups determined, and evaluated for any illnesses. The good healthy ones are protected and cared for and even pampered. They will be taken up for organ removal if they match with the client. If necessary, they would even be sacrificed."

"My God!"

"The captives are used as sources for organ transplantations for the wealthy for a price. If a certain individual is in need of a kidney, liver, or heart, the matched individual is either operated or sacrificed, and the necessary organ is removed and used. There are occasions when the organ is shipped to a certain hospital in need. There is a price for the organ, however. The donor is expendable in the island, but profits are assured for the laboratory."

"Do you conduct transplantation-related experiments?"

"Yes, we do. You may have heard about a recent trial done at New York University, where a genetically modified pig kidney was implanted in a human. The kidney worked very well for several days. Another news was a genetically modified pig heart was transplanted successfully to a human at University of Maryland."

"Does that open the door for easy availability of genetically modified organs procured from pigs or humans that do not face rejection?"

"That is true. We are also involved in this type of genetic research but using human experimentations. There is a possibility that a one-time genetic modification will be a better recourse instead of lifelong immune suppression drugs."

"Why human experimentations?"

"The best way to know if something will work or not is by doing human experimentations instead of wasting time on pigs and rats. The unhealthy captives are segregated and kept in separate cages for this purpose."

"What is the biggest human experimentation that is going on here now?"

"Brain transplantation is an ongoing experiment. Instead of opening the skull and removing the brain, which will necessitate cutting of all the nerves, blood vessels, and messing up with the soft brain, the trial is on removing the whole head along the lower part of the neck and transplanting the entire head, otherwise called as total head transplantation (THT)."

"How did they get this idea?"

"This concept has been described in ancient times. The Hindu god Ganesha is worshipped widely in India and other parts of the world. He is called as the elephant god because he has the head of an elephant. The story is that his head got cut off by mistake, and the supreme Lord replaced his head with that of an elephant who happened to be nearby. The infant god Ganesha survived and lived long. Egyptians had several gods with head of crocodiles, lions, and snakes."

"Any other stories from the past?"

"Another old Hindu epic story narrates an incident of transection of human heads and reattachments thereafter. A saint by the name of Jamadagni was infuriated with his wife because she had fleeting thoughts of infidelity when she saw a handsome demigod. So he asked his son Parasuraman to cut off her head as punishment. As he approached to behead his mother, another lady and her husband tried to protect her. So he cut the heads off all three individuals. He reported this to his father, who was very pleased with the loyalty of his son. It is very rare to find a son who will agree to cut off his own mother's head. Parasuraman asked for a boon from his father as a return favor. Jamadagni agreed to it. Parasuraman wanted to reattach the heads and make his mother alive again. Jamadagni told him to place the heads tight against the bodies, perform certain rituals and recitations, and squirt the holy water from his jug. Parasuraman went back to the site of killings and performed the steps as ordained. However, in his hurry, he placed the head of his mother against the body of the other lady and placed the lady's head against his mother's body. To the surprise of everyone, all three decapitated individuals came alive, except for the fact that his mother's head was switched to another lady's body and vice versa. He went back to his father explained the mistake. Jamadagni replied that they are now cursed to live like this and it is their destiny and that the switching cannot be undone."

"Still, why interchange the whole head instead of just the brain itself?"

"In case of other organ transplants such as heart and kidney transplants, the whole organ with blood supply is replaced instead of parts of the organ. So is the case for brain transplantation. It is better to transplant the entire head at the level of the neck instead of opening the skull and removing the brain. Opening the skull is a complicated deal with so many nerve endings and blood vessels. The brain is soft and pulpy. It will spill and break up on trying to remove the brain from the skull."

"Tell us more about the techniques in this type of surgery."

"The head is transected sharply along the intervertebral space between the sixth and seventh cervical vertebra so that the transection is below the bifurcation of the carotid artery across the common carotid artery. Trachea and upper esophagus are also transected. Spinal cord is glued together, bone is stabilized, and then the anastomosis is done between the common carotid artery, internal jugular vein, trachea, and esophagus. Vagus and phrenic nerves are attached at the end. The key is to avoid handling of soft brain tissue and all of the intricate nerve and blood vessel connections inside the skull. Instead, it is better to replace whole head."

"Do you have to work very fast since the brain can die in four minutes without oxygen?"

"Yes, the transplantation of brain must be done within four minutes of severing the original and transplanted head, since anoxic brain damage can occur by that time. This can be prolonged to ten minutes with induced hypothermia by running ice-cold solutions through the veins, keeping the body in cold temperature, and performing the procedure in arctic-cold atmosphere. A perfect fit between the transected spinal cords is done with the help of glue, immediately followed by stabilization of the vertebral column again with help of glue and nails. The common carotid artery and internal jugular veins are anastomosed with the help of intraluminal staples threaded into place via long catheters from distal parts of the body by a separate second team specialized in intravascular stapled anastomosis. This much can be done under ten minutes. What remains is only the reconnection of trachea and pharynx, nerves and muscles. Finally, the skin is closed. The entire procedure can be completed in less than thirty minutes."

"Such an operation must be a very big deal, never done so far in the world."

"Total head transplantation (THT) is by itself a big procedure. The procedure has never been done so far. Without human experimentation in a covert setting, it will never take off as a valid procedure. The setup needs advanced technology, expert physicians and surgeons, and trained paramedical personnel. Funding is needed in huge amounts. Without the help of underground money and capital support of large corporations and money launderers, it cannot be sustained. Unwanted and forgotten people are captured from around the world and held as prisoner guinea pigs in high-security sheltered cabins. They are fed and nourished to make sure they have good health."

"What is the market for head transplantation?"

"It is quite big indeed. Think of all the brain-dead individuals from gunshot wounds, automobile accidents, suicide attempts, infections, drowning, and other accidents and neurological disorders. How about treating dementia, Alzheimer's disease, and motor neuron disorders with THT?"

"Are there different types of head transplantation?"

"Single THT is done when a wealthy young person is brain-dead but could live a normal life if only the brain would function again. Most likely such a person is on life support and on ventilator and given intravenous fluids and well nourished. The patient is medical airlifted to the island hospital, and a donor head is obtained from one of the detainees who will be sacrificed after harvesting the head.

"Double THT is done as experiment and practice when two detainees are used. Their heads are cut off and switched simultaneously and reattached at the same time as double operation procedures set up side by side. Another experiment for practice is to cut off and reattach the same person's head. In this case, no tissue matching is needed. It is just to practice the operative techniques."

"What about controlling bleeding from all the cut blood vessels?"

"One major step in the operation is control of bleeding from the transected blood vessels and reattachment of them very quickly. As a preliminary step, balloon-tipped catheters are introduced to the origin of both common carotid arteries and both internal jugular veins. As soon as the head is transected sharply, the balloons are inflated to stop the forward bleeding. Vertebral arteries on both sides are clipped or ligated. Intraluminal microstaple-loaded catheter is advanced from proximal to distal end of the transected arteries, and the anastomotic staples are fired, and all four vessels are reattached, working from both sides as a double team."

"Are there any tricks to buy more time in conducting the operation?"

"Biostasis is a process to slow down cell degeneration. Tissues are allowed to go into metabolic hibernation by injecting the body part with a solution that would preserve it for an extended period of time. The solution pretends to be the blood circulating in a normal body. Along with the use of hypothermia, the body part can be reattached or transplanted at a convenient time instead of rushing the job. A scientific experiment was done in which decapitated animals from the butcher shop were infused with the special solution, and brain activity was noted even after four hours. Normally, anoxic brain death would have occurred after four minutes."

"What is the expected behavior of the brain-transplanted person?"

"This is indeed a very valid and challenging question. The brain controls all the emotions, intelligence, memories, and conduct of a person. The body has nothing but a mechanical function, as commanded by the brain. So the question is, who is this newly brain-transplanted person? Is it the brain getting a new body, or is it the old body getting a new brain? We assume that it is the brain that is all-important, and the new person behaves like the donor of the brain."

"So if a wealthy person wants to resurrect his son or daughter following sudden brain death, after brain transplant surgery, they will be getting the same body but a totally different person at the end?"

"That is correct. One may decide this is not a worthwhile project when seen from that perspective"

"Is this all legal or ethical?"

"One can embark on a debate whether this type of organization should be allowed to exist, whether this type of research should be allowed to proceed with their work. Is this legal? Definitely the answer is no. Is it moral? The answer is in your viewpoint. Is this a necessary venture? The answer is yes. The science must progress. Discoveries must be made. On one side, many millions of people are going to be cured of their diseases, many children are going to be free of their congenital disorders, people are going to live longer with better health. On the other side, some humans are going to be sacrificed. But then they were written off from the earth already, considered to be unwanted or dead. So why not use them to serve a purpose for the benefit of mankind? Think about it as a war, many soldiers will be sacrificed for the kingdom. Millions and millions of people have been killed in the name of wars. Society accepts such mass murders. So why not make use of a few destitute starving and neglected ones for advancement of science?"

Chapter 19

The Transformations

"We heard that experiments are being done here to transform behavior pattern of individuals. Is that true?"

"Who told you that?"

"We ran into one of your patients with his nurse. We ended up in a casual conversation with limited information."

"Yes, it is one of the experiments being done here."

"What is the methodology used?"

"They are trying gene therapy to modify behavior pattern of individuals. This is supposed to be a secretive project."

"Why is it so secretive?"

"The US government is involved in some of these experiments."

"What is involved in this technology?"

"Many disorders which are not correctable by drugs are now being treated by gene therapy. One such problem involves neurological and psychological disorders."

"How does it apply to people?"

"Mental disorders such as schizophrenia, bipolar disorder, and manic depressive psychosis are now treated with certain medications but never cured. With gene therapy, one-time treatment can make them calm and quiet on a permanent basis."

"Why is the US government involved in this?"

"They want to know if the terrorists with violent behavior can be converted to calm and peace-loving citizens."

"That would be something new."

"Yes. Instead of keeping them in jail such as Guantanamo Bay for indefinite number of years, they can be transformed to peaceful individuals."

"That should save a lot of money and effort."

"More than that, they can be sent back to their own home countries after treatment. They would preach peace and nonviolence this time instead of planning another terrorist attack."

"Are there any animal models on this type of work?"

"There is proof of genetically altered mosquitoes that do not transmit viral diseases. These treated mosquitoes even kill the untreated and harmful mosquitoes."

"It is clever to treat a terrorist with gene therapy, alter their mental state, convert them to be harmless, and send them back to their hometowns. There they will preach nonviolence and peace. They will stand against further violence or bombings or other terrorist activities. The followers will be astounded to see change in attitude of their leaders."

"What has been the result so far?"

"It is too early to tell. It seems to be working on certain situations."

"Do you find this technology applicable in medical practice?"

"Yes. Many of the psychosomatic conditions, neurological disorders, and degenerative conditions will be treated by gene therapy in the future."

"What about managing criminals and inmates who are in the jails?"

"There is so much money to be saved and efforts reduced by treating criminals by medical means rather than the current way of incarcerating them. Currently, as they are released from jails, they go on to continue committing the crimes. Some of them are serial killers who get back to their killing spree. They have become hardened criminals. With the new method of medical or genetic therapy, they can be sent back to the society much sooner. There they have become altered, mellow, and soft as better citizens."

"So this will be the future?"

"Yes. There will be fewer wars, less terrorism, less criminals. We convert the rapists and murderers to become normal citizens."

"So we can make a new slogan, 'Genes instead of jails!'"

"We are already sending mentally unstable criminals to psychiatric institutions instead of jails."

"So the judge can send these violent and irrational criminals for gene therapy?"

"Yes. It will be court-ordered gene therapy!"

"Has there been any previous scientific work on this field in the past?"

"Many years ago, they tried to do frontal lobotomy by surgery to convert mad people to sedentary nonviolent people. It was not a well-received step, since it carried many complications. The procedure was abandoned in favor of medications."

Chapter 20

The Services

"How do they get all these tasks done by providing worldwide services and maintaining extensive contacts?"

"It is mostly through the Dark Web Site, also known as DWS."

"How can one access it?"

"It has three separate portals. One is for exclusive rich clients, one for employees and hospitals and other health-care services, and last one for patients or clients."

"What are the benefits for the wealthy clients who become members of the DWS?"

"One of the perks for a member of DWS is the ability to request and get services that will be otherwise impossible to get. But of course, there is a price for everything. If you can pay, you can get anything done. That is the way the world runs. At times, return services will be expected instead of payment in cash. The wheel must run smoothly. It is like a mafia operation except it is done on digital format instead of in-person closed meetings."

"Give me an example of such services."

"The services offered or requested are unique and unusual and often illegal. It can be to get ammunition and guns for a certain group of people. It can be to eliminate the existence of certain individual with no trace. It can be to hire a child for labor or prostitution. It can be to win a political favor to benefit a certain corporation or individual. It can be to sell drugs and narcotics or money laundering. It can be to use the World Genetic Research Laboratory for DNA or genetic analysis. At times, it can be to manipulate the world stock market or currency value. It can be to rig the outcome of a sporting event or an election."

"How does the member request for a service?"

"A member usually makes the initial contact requesting service help through the website. Subsequently that person gets a reply from an anonymous service provider asking for further information. Then they make further contacts privately outside the DWS. However, every move, conversation, and action is somehow known to the network of DWS. Once the request is approved and a provider is established, then they make further negotiations on details as to when and where and the cost and methodology. From this point onward, it becomes a no-return situation. Any bad-faith actions or cheating or noncompliance will be met with death or other severe punishment."

"How are assassinations carried out with the help of DWS?"

"Charlie Windsor is in charge of assassination plots. He is a retired army major, tough on the outside as well as on the inside. He has no emotions, no humane feelings, and is single. He functions as a machine 'round the clock. Planning complex assassinations and executing them without a flaw is his excitement in life. It is a sport that he enjoys. The power, resources, and money are available in abundance. He has full authority to recruit assistants or hitmen as needed. A mercenary is an armed civilian recruited to conduct a military-style operation. Failure is not tolerated. All evidences must be erased instantly.

"For example, the president of a certain country wanted his own half brother to be eliminated. He was a real threat to his position as the president and dictator. So he arranged the job through the DWS for payment of $1 million. As the targeted person was coming out of an airplane, a lady accidentally rubbed against him and smeared his body with an ointment. It was a strong poison that got absorbed through his skin and made him extremely sick within twenty-four hours. He died the following day in the hospital despite all medical treatments. It was, however, declared as a natural death due to a viral illness.

"The president of another country wanted to get rid of his political enemy, who was running for election against him. So he arranged the job to be done through DWS. The targeted person was poisoned with his food at the hotel where he stayed after campaigning. He became violently sick and went into multiple organ failure the next day. Again he was taken to the hospital and was declared dead. In both of these instances, the corresponding state presidents sent condolences and wreath to the funeral. The media and the press declared these as accidental deaths."

"Did they help in sabotaging Iranian nuclear plants?"

"A secret meeting had been set up in Bermuda between three foreign secretaries of state on a Sunday at lunchtime. The plan was to sabotage the nuclear factory in Iran using cyberattack. None of them wanted to be involved directly. They had agreed to contact DWS, which in turn offered a contact person from one of those countries."

"How much money was paid for the job?"

"DWS did not accept money for this work but wanted a return job favor to be carried out by an Israeli agent. The return payment was in the form of assassination of vocal critic of President Nicholas Wood. This political opponent was planning a vacation sail in the Mediterranean next month. A sniper was arranged to do the job while his speedboat was passing close to a sailboat."

"How are payments arranged by the governments without raising questions?"

"Here are some examples. DWS was going to be paid in huge compensation for jobs already carried out. Money for all expenses and compensations for workers were to be met in the form of a corporate loan from the government. The government had allocated $1 trillion to help ailing businesses during the downturn of economy due to the COVID-19 pandemic. Several billion dollars of this money had been unaccounted for. Some of these funds were given to fake corporations that existed only in paper. On top of this, several of the loans were officially forgiven, since the businesses did not do well despite the loan. It was declared that the business failed for no fault of the organization. It was accepted that the lockdown from the coronavirus pandemic caused the catastrophe. The money was then ferreted out to do the nefarious tasks through DWS. While many people perished in the pandemic, many corporations and wealthy individuals flourished."

"Are you proposing that some of the recent assassinations that received publicity were coordinated through DWS?"

"A top nuclear scientist of Iran was assassinated in November 2020. His name was Mohsen Fakhrizadeh, who was responsible for the major nuclear development in Iran. It is suspected that Israel and the USA had a hand in it even though no one would admit it or no one would come forward to take the credit. Another Iranian military leader by the name of Qasem Soleimani was assassinated last year. Mr. Soleimani was a popular person and was credited with helping with the reformation of ISIS. Unknown assassins carried out these killings. Much of the groundwork was done through DWS. They denounce the DWS but at the same time keep it alive to do their dirty work. DWS makes good money and wields clout on both sides. Iranian leader Hassan Rouhani has promised retaliation and revenge. The big irony is that this will also be coordinated through DWS.

"Also alleged this time was that someone had ordered poisoning of a political opponent of a Russian president. He was poisoned through a nerve agent that was smeared on the inside of his underwear. It was designed to kill him. However, he barely escaped because the airplane in which he was traveling had to be diverted due to engine problems and it landed prematurely. Also, when he felt sick, immediate medical attention was provided to him on the ground."

"Give us some other scenarios where DWS was helpful?"

"Drone-operated unmanned flying devices have become secret weapons to carry portable nuclear weapons in addition to taking surveillance photographs and delivering packages to remote areas. They are used to deploy bombs on the terrorist camps in Afghanistan, hidden in the mountains. The drone technology is developed by a drone manufacturing company located in Kansas City, USA, and is kept as a high-secret intelligence development by the Pentagon. Pakistan wanted to steal the technology to work against India and across its borders. The high ranges of Himalayan mountains are unreachable six months of the year due to weather conditions. Pakistan arranged a bright IT student to study at MIT with full scholarship. He was to take drone technology as his major and was to visit the Kansas City plant as part of his thesis. He took many secret videos and pictures of the facility and the manufacturing process and codes. DWS assisted the process at the request of the Pakistani government for a hefty fee."

"Do they help with crime detection by doing DNA analysis?"

"DNA analysis has resolved many mystery cases. In all these cases of DNA analysis, standard STR technique, mitochondrial DNA analysis, and Y chromosome analysis have helped solve the problem of identification. The World Genetic Research Laboratory is well equipped to provide such services. It is estimated that ten thousand persons are wrongly convicted of their crimes every year in the USA alone. Worldwide, it could be in hundreds of thousands, especially in countries where legal recourse is unpredictable, system is corrupt, and politics and money play the role.

"Identity of a person is often difficult if the dead body is badly damaged following disasters. Airplane crashes, fire accidents, and other natural disasters leave behind charred, mutilated, and washed-off bodies. World Trade Center was knocked down on the 9-11 incident with over three thousand bodies, some severely damaged. DNA analysis of the remains served as a vital clue in personal identification. No one is better suited than the World Genetic Research Laboratory to conduct advanced studies on DNA and other gene-based evaluations."

"How about hacking other systems? Is DWS involved in this type of work?"

"Yes. Hacking can be done by seemingly unexpected ways. Tiny microscopic cameras are set up in electrical outlets, phones, ceiling fans, smoke alarms, flowers, screws in any location from doors to windows, closet hooks, shower gels, water bottles, clothes, buttons, hats, handbags, and furniture. Valuable information is obtained, and continued monitoring and surveillance is done for several days with video recording, along with still photographs. Russia was considered to have initiated one of the biggest computer hacks of the US government in December of 2020. It compromised a large volume of information involving defense, infrastructure, and environmental plans.

THE CLINIC

"Another major event was when Russia influenced or interfered with the US election in 2016. Russia wanted to have a certain individual to be elected. The affair was kept secretive, so they initiated a planned and progressive assault against the opponent. The campaign was effective. When a lie is told repeatedly and over and over with conviction, everyone starts believing that it is true.

"Another example of successful hacking was against Colonial Pipeline company along the Northeast Corridor in the USA on May 9, 2021, by a hacker named Dark Side. It effectively shut off gasoline supply to nearly half of the country for over a week. The company paid a ransomware of several million dollars when the hackers reset the computer system. A similar operation was conducted against beef industry later in the year, which caused beef prices to shoot up. Gas prices went up. FBI confirmed that there was a dark website involved in this activity.

"Analysts state that similar ransomware attacks are happening several times a year by the hackers who demand ransom, and they get away with it. It is estimated that over one thousand corporate hackings happen every year. Several million dollars are being paid as ransom every year. These hackers are hiding deep, often with the support of their local governments. They are careful not to attack health-care facilities. They demand ransom ahead of time, and there is nothing much anyone can do, including the US government, to thwart such attacks."

"Who initiates these conversations and interactions?"

"High-level people or governments through intermediaries request the services. The job is organized and conducted by DWS in a very quiet and discreet way. Everything is kept secretive. A price is levied. No one takes responsibility. They need an organization like DWS to do their dirty work. The World Genetic Research Laboratory and the World Fertility and Genetic Clinic are part of the same network."

Chapter 21

The Money

"There must be a lot of money that is rolling through this conglomerate with the World Fertility and Genetic Clinic, World Genetic Research Laboratory, and the Dark Web Site all functioning well."

"Absolutely. Everything revolves around money. On this planet, all characters, people, organizations, and governments play their parts based on money. It is what determines the actions and thoughts, policies and procedures. Education and career, family and children, vacation and fun all depend on it. Food on the table, shelter and roof, buying clothes and groceries—everything needs money. People respect those who can afford them and have money. They mock those who cannot afford the luxuries and who remain poor. Success is determined by the amount of money one has acquired, along with other parameters. In this real world, it would be bad luck if one has no money."

"How is the money transacted?"

"DWS collects huge amounts of money through various channels as payment for services or products. The bigger task is to keep it safe and launder it for further use. One legitimate use is to run the fertility clinics in multiple locations across the globe and interconnect them. This provides the network with a frontage to the public. Money is needed to acquire drugs and weapons, conduct human trafficking, and carry out assassinations. The World Genetic Research Laboratory is a valuable asset by itself. It runs world-class research that would be impossible in any country. The turnover is in millions of dollars each day. A whole group of employees is dedicated to follow the money trail. They are very good at it. DWS spends unlimited amounts to carry out a service or activity, since the reputation of the organization depends on the reliability and result. They cannot afford a sloppy service.

"Transactions are made either through online secure sites or in person. Banks in multiple locations in the Caribbean islands or in Europe act as the agents between the sender and the recipient. They are just holding agents. The money is then transferred to undisclosed locations across the globe either by wire transfer or by in-person pickup."

"We hear about alternative currency method such as cryptocurrency being used. Bitcoin is one such example. Is it being used in your system?"

"True. A new development in the financial world is the digital currency in different forms. Bitcoin is one example. There are other forms of digital transactions where no one sees any physical currency."

"How do you account for all these types of transactions?"

"Irrespective of how it is conveyed, every penny that needs to be collected is collected, and all expenses are accounted for."

"How do they legitimize the expenses?"

"Nonprofit organizations are good ways to collect money and spend them without much accounting or legalities. No taxes are paid, as they are nonprofit. Managers can skim the money and spend it for personal needs with very little attention paid by others except the insiders."

"Tell us an example on this."

"An example is Build the Wall organization that was supposed to help build a wall at the southern border of the United States to reduce the asylum seekers from Mexico. They collected $25 million and showed that they spent $24 million of it in a period of three years. An actual wall built was less than a mile. The rest went to management expenses."

"There must be a lot of expenses to run this operation here."

"The World Genetic Research Laboratory has huge expenses. There is genuine research that is not permitted legally in any of the countries. Numerous scientists and employees have to be paid and given room and board. Separate living quarters have to be maintained for captive humans, cloned organs or individuals, and animals that are needed for experiments. Modern equipment, full hospital facility, full operating room facility, and modern state-of-the-art laboratory are made available. They have to be met with adequate income. Entire supplies, food, and provisions for the Lab Island are imported for daily sustenance.

"The expenses across the globe are also mind-boggling. Each and every transaction has to be paid off. Clinics that collect specimens and organs have to be reimbursed. Service coordinators who perform the jobs must be paid. Travel, accommodation, and incidental expenses must be met. Laundering the black money and converting illegal money to white money is a project by itself. Digital currency, cryptocurrency, and DWS have made these transactions quite easy and untraceable.

"Whenever possible, DWS arranges payments or paybacks as return services instead of going through cash transactions. For example, one member requests a certain service. That member is then asked to perform another task instead of paying for the service."

Chapter 22

The Recruitment

"How do you get these scientists and other workers to come here and work?"

"Scientists are held at highest esteem at the World Genetic Research Laboratory. They are actively recruited from all over the world, offered with all sorts of incentives. There is a recruitment wing of the organization always on the lookout for suitable employees."

"What criteria are used to recruit them?"

"Race, religion, color, or sex does not matter. What matters is their intelligence and inquisitive nature. They are known for their quest for research, hard work, dedication, and paranoia."

"What attracts them to come here?"

"Sometimes they have been ignored or unrecognized in their field. They may have had difficult personalities because of their focus for perfection. Often they were not the most likable colleagues. They offend others easily because they are often working at different wavelength than others. They are not 'nice' and they do not do small talks. They are misunderstood as being rude or harsh or stuffy or selfish. They often feel dejected for one reason or another."

Stephen Lander is in charge of recruitment for the Lab Island. He is a retired CEO of a Fortune 500 company. He is in charge of the entire residents and workers in the Lab Island. It is a complicated process to identify suitable candidates, have them accept the job, sign the contract, and keep them working here. Their life during the work and afterward have to be monitored closely.

Once a suitable person is identified as a potential recruit, the DWS would try anything possible to recruit that person.

"Is it the salary that attracts them?"

"No. Surprisingly it is not money that attracts the scientists."

"Then what is it?"

"It is the freedom and amenities to do what they want and how they want and when they want so that they can quench their thirst for discovery and advancements in science. That is their adrenaline and endorphin flow. Such experiments are forbidden due to regulations and oversight in all other countries."

"Why can't they do it in their own country?"

"They could be very expensive experiments and may need excellent infrastructure. There is so much bureaucracy, nepotism, cronyism, protocols, rules, regulations, and corruption in usual workplaces."

World Genetic Research Laboratory offers total freedom, amenities, staffing, and equipment to do what they want to do. Money and salary are offered at a level more than any other place. Results matter here and not the methods or means.

"Did they have personal problems in previous workplaces?"

"Some of these brilliant minds are considered criminals in the civilized world, since they have broken the laws. They have been forbidden from conducting future experimentations. They cannot get a respectable job in the universities any longer. Their peers consider their advanced theories as irrelevant or bizarre. They have conducted experiments considered as unethical or immoral by their administrators. Often their work is disapproved due to high cost and need for permits from governmental authorities. Some others have had other criminal records such as murdering their spouses or coworkers or tax evasions or theft. Some others have had history of sexual misconduct at work. The line between a lunatic and brilliant is very thin, and they themselves do not know when they are crossing the borders."

"What about support employees?"

"Second group of employees are assistants or facilitators to the scientists. For each scientist, there are at least three assistants appointed. Their job is to get everything facilitated, arranged, prepared for the scientists and assist in the actual conduct of the experiment the scientist wants to perform. They maintain logbooks and records. They interact with the administration and other scientists, schedule events, organize the experiments, record the results, and provide necessary follow-up evaluations, and communicate closely with their scientist."

"Still, there must be need for other workers."

"Then there are the infrastructure employees. They are the ground engineers, administrators, electricians, technology workers, security guards, first responders in emergencies, nursing staff for the hospital and operating theater, food and beverage workers, and transportations workers."

"What about nurses?"

"In the state of Kerala in South India, many low-income families encourage their girls to study nursing as their passport to job opportunities and income uplift. Nursing is a taboo in North India as a menial work. But there is a massive shortage of good nurses all over the world. Many Kerala nurses work all over the world. One of their hurdles is getting passport and visa. They also want income guarantee. The World Genetic Research Laboratory with its attached hospital entices them to work in the Lab Island with no hurdles."

"Are they paid well?"

"They are paid better than their income at home. The rewards are better than other countries. The entire salary can be saved and sent home. More than anything, the biggest incentive is that there is no need to obtain a visa."

"Who else?"

"Final groups are the lower-level workers such as errand peons, sweepers, sanitation and housekeeping workers, morgue managers, garbage disposal workers, food and beverage services, laundry services, and telephone operators. Many such employees are needed to conduct proper functioning of the World Genetic Research Laboratory and hospital. In other words, the Lab Island is like a city by itself with every sort of worker, as you would see in any other city."

"Where do you get these people to come from?"

"All these various employees are recruited from different countries. There is no specific location. English speaking and health-care education are desirable qualifications. Most of them come from Asian countries like India, Pakistan, Bangladesh, Sri Lanka, Vietnam, Cambodia, South Korea, to name a few. They also come from all of Europe and the USA."

"Once recruited, how do they come here?"

"They are flown in to the island from their homeland from the closest airport through Cuba. We pay for the full transportation and incidental expenses."

"Once they arrive here, what can they expect?"

"They are provided with accommodation, food, drinking water, and health care. They are well taken care of with no worries and no concerns. They are to focus on their work."

"How is their salary and benefits?"

"They are paid very good salary credited to their bank accounts of choice. They are fully provided for while at work in the island with no need for any cash. They have no expenses here. Even clothing is provided with appropriate type of uniforms, which differentiates their category of work. The entire salary can be totally saved in their account in the main land in their hometown."

"Tell us about the uniforms, and what does it indicate?"

"Lower-level workers wear brown/khaki, infrastructure employees wear blue colors, and assistants, nurses, and other health-care workers wear green, while scientists and top-level administrators wear whites."

"It appears that the island is self-contained."

"The island is somewhat similar to a cruise ship, self-contained in all living matters and lifestyle. The island is a city where life is free, work is unlimited and around the clock."

"What are the negatives?"

"Everyone is monitored and watched. No communication is allowed to the outside world. There is no internet, no television, no radio, and no postal service. Once you arrive the island, you can communicate with your colleagues and superiors but no other person, including your family or friends. The focus here is work, work, and work with no distractions."

"What is the minimum duration of contract?"

"Minimum duration of work is one year. After one year, they can have a break period of one month to go home or visit family or friends. That transportation expense is included in the benefit package. However, they are not allowed to discuss the work conditions or function of the island in any way with anyone. They will be watched closely during their vacation period also."

"What if someone falls ill or gets depressed or insists on leaving after a few months before one-year term ends?"

"They have a world-class hospital and doctors to treat all illnesses right here. They are not allowed to leave until their work term ends."

"Why would they want to continue to live and work here?"

"Take a look at the benefits for an ordinary employee who may have been starving with no food or shelter in his or her hometown. They are promised with a job assignment with a very lucrative salary with total coverage of all expenses and health benefits. The entire salary can be saved for their future. While recruiting, they are told that it is a job in the Caribbean Island, to work for a major research firm that includes a pharmaceutical laboratory and a hospital. For millions of people, it is an offer of a lifetime, a dream come true."

"What happens when they return to their homeland after the required term but do not want to come back for another term?"

"Those who elect to stop working for the World Genetic Research Laboratory are warned again to avoid discussing their job or work condition or facilities with anyone for at least five years after departure. They are monitored and closely followed without their knowledge. Any leaks or cheating will be met with severe punishment. Extreme secrecy of the island is protected at all cost."

Chapter 23

The Procurement

"So tell us how you get these captives."

"They are collected from all over the world. All of the humans held in captivity here are captured with the help of local people in third world countries."

"Why do you need these people, anyway?"

"The World Genetic Research Laboratory needs raw materials for its research. Human beings are the most wanted raw material for such experiments here."

"Why not do the usual types of clinical research?"

"When companies have to conduct clinical research, they request people to be volunteers. When volunteers are not available, they sometimes go to third world countries. They make promises of gifts or cure of illnesses."

"How about doing the experiments on animal models first?"

"They do a small number of experiments on animals and extrapolate the results to humans. Certain types of medical experiments need live animals such as pigs or rats, which may end up being sacrificed at the end. Activists and environmentalists raise objections even for this. Stem cell research was banned in USA at one time because of the moralists making an issue of using fetal tissue for such research."

"But there is nothing like using humans for the live experiments. Why go through indirect tracts when a direct method can be made possible?"

"How is it possible to capture these people?"

THE CLINIC

"Robert Strickowsky is the person in charge of procurement for the Lab Island. This involves procuring humans, animals, and other supplies for the experiments and for day-to-day functioning of the island."

"How about importing necessary provisions for the island?"

"A long network of agents and supply chains are maintained for this specific purpose. Provisions and food items as well as medicines and health-care items are also imported. All necessary food and supplies are imported. Nothing much is grown or manufactured in this island."

"What is the justification for capturing human beings like this?"

"There are thousands of humans who die needlessly all over the world. Some of them are running away from crime-ridden areas or war-torn neighborhoods or from famine and hunger or from neglected or abused families. There are over sixty million refugees every year looking for a safe haven, for better opportunities, for better life. Many are running away from dictators who are responsible for genocide. There are riots, bigotry, and abuse. Race and religion are used to discriminate against each other. Hundreds of homeless people are sleeping in the streets in every major city. People go missing all the time with no trace of them.

Over forty thousand people are being murdered every year in the USA alone from gun violence, and over seventy thousand are dying from suicide every year. Millions of people are being killed in the name of wars. There are hundreds of boys and girls who are running away from home or committing suicide because of abusive stepfathers and stepmothers. Why not use some of them who do not want to live anymore? How about taking some of the hard-core criminals in the overcrowded prisons who are likely to come out of jail by legal measures soon and will continue to perpetrate their criminal activities again?"

"How about police or family members looking for them?"

"It is a possibility. However, most of them have been given up for good. Truth is that they are not missed and no one is looking for them."

"Still, is it morally right to do so?"

"If a certain individual is starving, with no shelter or clothes, cannot find food or cover over the heads, and has become desperate to try anything, the recruiters of the World Genetic Research Laboratory are godsent, who offer great benefits. These individuals are carefully picked up, given food and shelters, treated nicely, and given best follow-up care. Eventually they are shipped over to the Lab Island, where again they are treated nicely. They are kept comfortable and happy. They are even provided with a partner for sex. A medical team examines them, takes blood tests, and other medical tests, including x-rays."

"What do you do with them eventually?"

"If they are in good health, a day may come when they are given a sedative, taken to the operating room to harvest an organ for someone who is rich. It could be the day when they are taken for experimental surgery such as head transplantation. If it is a woman, she may be allowed to become pregnant in the island, only to have her fetus removed to harvest germ cells. Or she may be asked to be a surrogate mother for a genetically modified baby undergoing in-vitro fertilization."

"Still, is it morally right to sacrifice them for organs or experiments?"

"We raise cattle, fish, chicken and make them well grown and kill them for meat. We raise genetically modified plants, crops, and other agricultural products to harvest them for our consumption. We can extrapolate the same concept on humans also."

"Is there a gender preference for the captives?"

"Both men and women are needed for the laboratory for various needs. We also need a certain number of children."

"How do you safeguard them?"

"The captured individuals are precious properties and are safeguarded in high-security shelters as secure as maximum-security prisons with continuous remote cameras, monitoring of every conversation, high walls with electric wire protection, and individual cells. They are kept in the same way as keeping cattle before butchering them, well fed and well maintained."

"Tell us some examples when people were taken as captives."

THE CLINIC

"Nigerian jihadists kidnapped over three hundred boys, similar to three hundred girls kidnapped a few years ago by Boko Haram. This time, it was the jihadists of the same Boko Haram who went into an all-boys' boarding school in Katsina, northern part of Nigeria, to punish them for 'un-Islamic practices.' One of the students who escaped stated that a platoon of soldiers with guns ordered the entire school to march through forest, threatening to kill anyone who did not obey or tried to escape. A total of 333 boys were found missing. Abubakar Shekau is the most wanted terrorist in Africa, with a $7 million bounty on his head as the leader of the terrorist group.

"A Canadian tycoon from the fashion industry by the name of Peter Nygard faces charges for years of sex trafficking and racketeering. Dozens of victims in the US, Canada, and the Bahamas are involved. He controlled the victims usually captured from poor backgrounds with threats or false promises of jobs or promotion."

"Does the Dark Web Site help in this procurement?"

"Yes, DWS has a large network of helpers and employees all over the world that would help in the process of procurement. Some of them are already employees of the World Fertility and Genetic Clinic, some others are employees of DWS. Many others are contract workers of mercenary nature. They are paid per job or per hour and expenses. They are to scout for suitable persons. They keep a low profile, prey on their victims, and entice them to join them for a better life. Rarely ever do they use violence to recruit them. Instead, they lure them with promise of food, shelter, and clothing. They end up as procured products unwittingly."

"This whole thing is obnoxious and immoral."

"It depends on one's point of view. Thousands of people are being murdered under one pretext or another all over the globe every year. If a certain of them can help advance medical science and help save lives of other fellow humans or help cure certain diseases, why would it be wrong?"

Chapter 24

The Progress

Treatment protocols of Nora Gerber and Nicki Pappas went fairly smooth. They did not require any open surgery but did involve small-puncture procedures. This was to remove blood cells from the umbilical cord of the fetus, treat the blood, and reinfuse them with the modified blood from a genetic point of view. Still, it was a very scary procedure, interfering with the blood supply of the growing fetus.

"How did our treatments go, doctor? Is there a hope for success?" They were anxious to know.

"We are pretty certain that Nicki's problem of thalassemia in the baby was going to be corrected."

"What about Nora and the baby with Down syndrome?"

"We are not fully sure about correcting Down syndrome in Nora's baby. We have done our best to edit the chromosome 21, to remove the extra chromosome in it. But we need to check it again after the baby is born."

They were in the island for one week all together. They were allowed to return to their home state in the USA, with follow-up with the World Fertility and Genetic Clinic in Los Angeles. Don and John had spent the week talking to so many different people at the island and had gotten a lot of information. They were indeed transformed. They were admiring the work and dedication by the scientists and were convinced about the need for such good work.

It was time for them to return. They had made full payments for the services. Helicopter ride was arranged to take them back to Havana in Cuba, where they will stay for two days. The helicopter ride over the ocean was scary, with no way of knowing the directions. The pilot knew his whereabouts. Once again, they had to fill out a whole bunch of forms and go through formalities to get back to the USA. After completing immigration papers and approval, they took the flight back to California.

Rani and Sooraj met them at the airport. They were thrilled to meet them, since there was no communication that was allowed from the island. They took them to Rani's house for dinner. They wanted to know all about their experiences and wanted a detailed report. However, Don and John had been forewarned about disclosure and penalties. So they were careful in their conversations but conveyed the gist of their treatments and results. They were to meet at the next Lamaze class the following week.

In the meantime, they were reading about increasing incidences of cyberattacks and ransomware attacks, and all the nations wanted to take preventive steps to protect themselves.

National security advisers in different countries observed a pattern in hacking, extortions, illegal trades, and human trafficking. Scientists noticed subtle undisclosed but certain developments in genetic science and were alarmed about human experimentation. They reported these findings to their seniors and then forwarded them to their governmental agencies. Western media mostly blamed Russia and China for the rogue activities. But the insiders knew about DWS and the World Genetic Research Laboratory. Secret communications were underway between participating nations and allies.

Motion was made in the United Nations Security Council to exhort all nations to take collective steps in preventing cyberattacks. The US government increased budget allocation to fight cybercrimes. They declared that cyberattacks would be treated as terrorist attacks. Key player nations agreed to clamp down on the same, but they were soul-searching, since they were part of the rogue group themselves. So they were not going to do anything serious, except for the media talk and media condemnation. They would be happy to see the power of DWS diminished, but they were prime users of the website themselves. They needed the help of an anonymous middle person to do their dirty work. It was suspected that the heads of nations such as USA, Russia, Iran, Israel, Saudi Arabia, China, Libya, Palestine, Lebanon, Afghanistan, and Pakistan were regular users of the site, but there was never a direct proof.

Similarly, the type of research that was being done as well as the services being provided was felt to be valuable and much needed. If we don't do it, someone else is going to do it. The future lies on genetic therapy to stop many different congenital and inherited disorders to treat many different diseases, to prolong longevity of humans, and even to save humanity from major disasters. Cancer treatments depend on further understanding of genetics and gene therapy. Many new drugs are going to depend on biotechnology and molecular biology. Look at the speed with which vaccines were manufactured to stop COVID-19 pandemic. There is a need to conduct unhinged, unregulated pure scientific research somewhere. Every nation will benefit from it eventually.

Rani, Nora, and Nicki went for the six-month checkup at the World Fertility and Genetic Clinic at Los Angeles. Rani had in-vitro fertilization, and Nora and Nicki had genetic therapy of the fetus. Fortunately, all three of them were progressing well with their pregnancy.

The doctor said, "The three of you have most precious babies you can think of. Two of you had genetic treatments done. Rani had difficult conceptions. So you need to take extra precautions."

"What should we do, doctor?"

"From now onward, you need medical checkups every two weeks at your local hospital and gynecologist. Watch your body weight and your diet. Take the prenatal vitamins. Have the blood pressure checked."

"Okay, doctor."

"It is necessary to avoid gestational diabetes, excess weight gain, and high blood pressure. Exercise and stress reduction is important. No alcohol and no smoking."

"Yes, doctor."

THE CLINIC

"One more important item. I would suggest that each of you consider having a cesarean section at the time of delivery instead of vaginal birth."

"Why?"

"Because these are precious babies. You do not want anything to go wrong with the delivery. A planned C-section at term is a lot safer in modern days. But it is up to you to decide whether you want a natural vaginal delivery or not."

"Do we have to check the babies for genetic issues after they are born?"

"Yes, absolutely they have to be checked. It is routine nowadays, anyway. A battery of genetic tests is done automatically for all newborn children in this country. It is a legal requirement."

"Moreover, Nora and Nicki had gene therapies done in utero. We have to know the results and report them to the World Genetic Research Laboratory. We also have to follow these children for several years afterward. We need your cooperation and help for the advancement of science and technology."

The three ladies walked out thinking about themselves and their babies. They made sure the babies were moving inside, smiled, and compared notes. They had lunch together before heading back to their homes.

Rani went back to her gynecologist, Dr. Meena, for routine prenatal visit. The nurse did a blood test and told her that her blood sugar was getting elevated.

Dr. Meena told her, "We need to be careful to keep the blood sugar in normal range. We shall repeat the tests again next week with fasting blood sugar and your body's utilization of the sugar level."

Next week, the blood sugar remained elevated in spite of it fasting blood sugar.

"I think you are having gestational diabetes."

"What does it mean, doctor?"

"You have to control this with better adjustment in diet, cutting back on carbohydrates, exercising more, and reducing any sugary drinks. I may have to prescribe some pills in addition."

"Is this going to be dangerous, doctor?"

"The baby can be bigger in size. You are likely to get diabetes in the future. But it is not dangerous as long as you keep a watch on it. We shall monitor your blood sugar levels every two weeks until the baby is out."

The blood tests on Nora and Nicki were normal. They became close buddies and hoping for good outcome and keeping their fingers crossed.

Chapter 25

The Delivery

Rani, Nora, and Nicki, all three of them were patients of Dr. Meena seeing her in her clinic and the attached hospital. All three of them had also been going to World Fertility and Genetic Clinic. All of them had agreed that the best place to have the delivery is with Dr. Meena and her hospital next door, which had full facilities to do the C-section.

After discussions with their husbands and their own soul-searching, all three opted for C-section.

Dr. Meena was happy to have three patients needing C-section under her care back-to-back within a few days apart. The hospital was also ready.

The nurse was in touch with them.

"You need to have your paperwork ready and set it up with the hospital at least a few days ahead of time."

"What is involved?"

"Don't worry. I shall give you a package for each of you to read and sign. It contains a consent form for doing the C-section, admission to the hospital, permission for administration of anesthesia and necessary medications, insurance forms, and a living will. Take your time, review everything, and return them to me. Feel free to ask any questions."

"What is this about living will?"

"Well, for you, it is just a formality. We are supposed to have it in file. If in case something is to go wrong and you are on life support, you are giving advanced directives as to life-prolonging measures."

"You don't expect us to become comatose as they showed in a movie."

"No, not at all. As I said, it is a formality, just a paper we are supposed to fill up for each and every patient who is admitted to the hospital for whatever reason. Don't take it seriously."

They had another visit with Dr. Meena for recheck.

"When is our surgery going to be scheduled?"

"We shall plan to do it as close to your expected due date, but it could be a day or two ahead of time based on the scheduling availability, doctor's availability, and your own preference."

"What do you mean by our own preference?"

"Sometimes patients request a certain day or time that they think is most auspicious for the baby to be born based on horoscope. Husband may want to be in the labor room based on his work schedule. Within reason, a few hours before or after is not going to change the outcome."

"Are you still recommending that we have C-section instead of vaginal delivery?"

"This issue had been discussed with you in the past. It would be your decision. If you decide to have a natural delivery, we would not object to it. However, there could be last-minute uncertainties compared to doing an elective planned C-section. This being a precious baby, you may want to be cautious."

"What could be such uncertainties?"

"The labor could be prolonged, since this is the first time or what we call as preemie. Premature rupture of the amniotic membrane can cause rush in labor. Sudden fetal distress can occur from cord compression. Some items such as placental position, fetal position, and outlet size we can predict. But there are situations that we cannot predict."

All three ladies nodded their heads in unison.

"We shall be doing another ultrasound next week to determine the status of the baby, the lay, the placenta, and the baby's life. You will also get to know the sex automatically."

They were all excited with four more weeks to go. They were having mixed feelings of joy and fear. They felt like crying and smiling at the same time. Will everything go all right? Can problems crop up suddenly? Will they get premature labor contractions? Will they get vaginal bleeding? Best thing is to pray and talk to parents over FaceTime. We must take the mind off and go by one day at a time.

They read up and reviewed the operation of caesarean section on Google. The general impression is that Julius Caesar was delivered by this method. However, this is unproven and is called to question. Some consider the word to have been derived from Latin words *caesones* or *caedere*, which means "cut open." About one-third of deliveries in the USA are done by caesarean section, while it is much lower in other countries. In ancient times, when the mother is full term and dies, they resorted to cutting open her abdomen in an effort to save the child.

Rani talked to the nurse again.

"What are some reasons for emergency C-section?"

"Nowadays, it is done when either mother or baby is having difficulties in safe delivery. Such reasons include delivery not progressing as expected, baby being in distress, baby being in abnormal position, multiple babies, placental problems, prolapsed umbilical cord, previous C-section, and health concerns of mother. While complications can happen during or after surgery, it is relatively safe in modern times."

"What type of anesthesia is given to us?"

"The procedure can be done under spinal or epidural regional block with sedation. Every so often they have to give general anesthesia. The anesthesia doctor will decide and will be there the whole time."

They had the ultrasound evaluation and blood tests and blood pressure checks on the following week. Everything appeared to be going well. Except for mild intermittent contractions, they were not experiencing any significant problems. They were scheduled for elective C-section in two- and three-week time. Preoperative paperwork and blood tests and anesthesia interviews were completed.

Rani had taken a laxative the night before. Nothing to eat or drink from midnight or as ordered as NPO from midnight. Surgery was scheduled for 8:00 a.m. She was admitted to the outpatient center by 6.00 a.m. The nurse went over the questions again, which Rani felt were silly.

"What is your name?"
"Why are you here?"
"Who is your doctor?"
"What operation are you having?"
"Did you eat or drink anything for past six hours?"
"Do you have any allergies?"
"Do you have a living will?"
"Who brought you here?"
"What medications are you taking?"
"Are you on any blood thinners?"

Then she started an intravenous line to give fluids and blood. She also put on an armband and prepared another armband for the baby.

A few minutes later, the anesthesia nurse walked in and went over her chart and asked more or less the same questions again and then asked her to open her mouth, put out the tongue, and asked breathe in and out while listening to her chest with a stethoscope. Then she explained that they would be giving her an epidural, which is an injection into the spinal canal in the back that would reduce her pain and sort of paralyze the lower half of the body, but she would be awake and know what was going on.

A few minutes later, the anesthesia doctor, who was a heavyset middle-aged man with a beard, walked in and told her that everything would be fine and asked if she had any questions. Rani did not know what to ask. She sort of drifted off as the doctor injected some medicine into her vein through the intravenous tube.

When Dr. Meena walked in a few minutes later, she had only a vague dreamlike memory. When she tried to talk to her, it was like being in a fog. She remembered that they held hands for a short duration, and she smiled. She felt that she was being moved smoothly and placed on a warm narrow bed by several hands. Then she fell asleep for a while.

When she woke up, she was hearing a lot of panic in the conversation between doctors and nurses. She could hear Dr. Meena literally screaming.

"Where the hell is the neonatologist? This was an elective case that everyone knew about!"

"He is on the way, madam."

"Hold the baby upside down, wipe the mouth, and tap the back. Make it cry, for God's sake!"

She heard a bustle of activities and then she heard the baby cry. It cried a little initially and then it started crying louder and harder.

Then she heard Dr. Meena screaming again.

"Get some blood transfusion going. Where the hell is the bleeding coming from? Give me the clamp and hold this high!"

Rani felt something was going wrong. It appeared the baby was alive, and she felt she was bleeding from somewhere. All she could do was close her eyes and pray to God. She could not feel any pain, but she could hear the conversations. Then something happened when the anesthesiologist injected some more medicine into her intravenous tube. She fell asleep again.

When she woke up, she was in her room. There was pain along the lower abdomen. She checked herself if she could move her legs and arms. They appeared to be weak and flabby, but there was some movement. She felt like passing urine. But the nurse told her she had a catheter in place and the urine was being removed through the tube on a continuous fashion. She told her to rest for a while.

Rani asked, "How is my baby?"

"Oh, he is fine. You have good-looking baby boy."

"When can I see him?"

"In a short while, when you are a bit more awake. He is healthy and weighs ten pounds."

The nurse went over and came back with her son. Sooraj had already seen him from the labor room. Rani was thrilled to hold him. She was full of smiles and happiness. All the pain and suffering disappeared in an instant.

Another nurse came over and asked for the name of the baby.

Rani said, "He is just born. We have not thought about a name."

"We must have a name as soon as possible. It is legally necessary before you can be discharged. Till then, he will be called Baby Sooraj."

Rani and Sooraj huddled and thought about a name. Finally, they agreed he would be named Aditya, meaning "the firstborn." They would call him Adi for short.

Three days later, she was discharged with instructions on follow-up care, wound care, and postnatal precautions. She was curious to know what happened to Nora and Nicki. They had also deliveries with C-section in the subsequent days. She was told that their surgeries went well and the babies were safe.

A few more days later, during the first visit with their pediatrician, they found out more about the final outcome of their gene therapy.

The pediatrician told Rani, "You are good to go. You are one lucky woman. Your baby looks great. He has no medical or genetic problems. He needs the next checkup in one month, and we shall give him the various shots soon."

"Thank you, doctor." She was all smiles and happy to hold him in her hands.

"Do you have any questions?"

"What should I feed him besides breast milk?"

The doctor went over various dietary instructions and referred her to talk to their neonatal nurse for further clarifications.

Nora was not lucky. Her baby was diagnosed of Down syndrome in the uterus and then had genetic therapy done at the World Genetic Research Laboratory. Her choice was to either have an abortion and start over or try for a gene therapy at the World Genetic Research Laboratory. She underwent the genetic therapy. The baby looked normal in appearance but was not completely normal on gene testing. The doctor warned that her baby girl might need close supervision in raising her.

Nora decided to raise the baby girl as a normal child and provide good support. The doctors thought that she would be able to grow up with some disabilities but would be able to learn and play with other children.

Nicki had a baby boy, and he also appeared normal. His genetic test report was good with no evidence of thalassemia in him. The genetic treatment at the World Genetic Research Laboratory for him was a total success.

All three of them were asked to go to the World Fertility and Genetic Laboratory for further evaluations and follow-ups. They remained friends and happy. Rani and Nora were planning to have a second child, while Nicki did not want to take any more chances. She felt lucky now and did not want to go through the travel to the Lab Island again. Once is enough.

Chapter 26

The Raid

Meanwhile, Don heard that there was a raid on the island laboratory. Several of the employees were quickly evacuated just prior to the raid. His cousin was among those who were evacuated. It was through him that he learned about the raid.

The cousin was now back home in Indianapolis after rapid evacuation.

"When did this take place?"

"It happened just a few days after you left. It was pitch dark, being a new moon night. The sky was very clear, with no chance of rain. Not even clouds. Stars were shining bright like diamonds sprinkled all over in the absence of moonlight. It was dead silent at 4:00 a.m. in the island. Only noise was that of the gentle waves hitting shores with ever so light breeze."

"How did they arrive?"

"Ten stealth helicopters each carrying ten commandos and ten speedboats carrying another ten commandos approached the island quietly. Very silently and very quietly, they landed and they ran out quickly with military precision as soon as the vehicles arrived."

"What did they do after landing?"

"The helicopter-based commandos had orders to get down by parachutes onto the top of the building, and speedboat commandos had orders to get down to the land as quickly as possible as they approached the island. The two hundred commandos had specific instructions to take control of the entire World Genetic Research Laboratory with minimal damage."

"Did they arrest anyone?"

"They were to capture the scientists, employees, and prisoners but not kill anyone unless there is an absolute need. They are to take control of the facility but not damage or destroy anything."

"Who made the decision to conduct the raid?"

"A consensus decision had been made between participating countries to conduct the raid on the Lab Island."

"What was the reason for the raid?"

"Several countries wanted to punish the DWS and World Genetic Research Laboratory because they had become too powerful. These countries had used their services on occasion in the past, but they were also fearful of exposure and scandal."

"What was their goal?"

"The plan was to make a surprise raid and attack, arrest all the scientists and employees, release all the captives, and stop all research work and take away all the computers and data."

"So this was preplanned?"

"It was a major preplanned attack."

"I am sure they did not want to destroy the scientific work."

"You are right. They were to preserve all scientific work and make sure there were no damages to the work in progress."

"Where they concerned about any particular items?"

"They were to be extra careful to prevent any release of virus or other contagious elements from the campus."

"How was the publicity controlled?"

"Major media publicity was given by the participating nations that a rogue terrorist activity has been destroyed and stopped. USA will take full credit for the surprise invasion, billed as an antiterrorist raid to help the world. The raid will be publicized as a successful mission to stop terrorism against the world. It will be announced that US-led commandos had taken over a secretive camp used by the terrorists, and their brain center had been permanently sabotaged."

"What did they find at the center?"

"The findings by the federal agents at the laboratory were mind-boggling. The main laboratory itself was a very well-equipped, a state-of-the-art genetics research center. There were many employees scuttling around wearing blue uniforms with masks and gloves. Some others were wearing full personal protection attire with impervious gowns, hoods, and spaceman-like suits, along with thick rubber gloves. They are the only ones allowed to open the storage compartments or remove their contents. Then there were a few at the desk and computer screens wearing white uniforms. They appeared to be the brains behind the projects.

"There were large screens with all sorts of displays of chromosomes, formulas, and cellular equations, which were constantly changing based on entries made by the professors or scientists. An array of laptops and computer desks that will match the NASA control desk was noted.

"There were large worktables with glass jars, pipettes, centrifuges, and solutions of different colors, various tubes, vials, chemicals, and scales. Electronic measurements were used to measure the tiniest of the droplets and weigh the lightest of lightest molecules. Measurement of vapors and mists and smoke was important to know the transmission and spread by air.

"Refrigerators and cold storages were critical. Large-sized walk-in cold storages as well as small-sized refrigerators were noted. Temperature can be controlled in these units from normal room temperature to ultracold freezers to minus a thousand degrees. At the same time, there were microwave heaters and warm storages noticed. Incubators of various sizes to grow cells, bacteria, fetus, sperms, and eggs were organized in a neat row. Tissues were being handled with extreme care and precautions to avoid spillage, leaks, or damage. Multiple autoclaves were present to sterilize instruments, glassware, and tubes."

"Did they find the laboratory set up to be well organized?"

"The structure of laboratory itself marveled any advanced center in the world. Everything was well organized, labeled, and easy to approach. Worktables and research desks were in one row. Control kiosks with array of computers were in the center of the room.

THE CLINIC

Display screens were large and visible from everywhere. Separate closed-off rooms with glass barriers were present for small and large conferences. Restrooms, food quarters and canteen, and soft-drink dispensers were in a different location. Smoking was not allowed anywhere. All precautions against fire hazard or contamination with virus or bacteria were undertaken. No cell phones, no internet, and no outside contact were permitted to prevent leaks and to maintain concentration and focus on work."

"Did they find the captives held for human experimentation?"

"On one side of the campus was a prison with proper personal care amenities and food for one hundred fifty men, equal number of women, and fifty children of various ages. They were held as captives for human experimentation such as organ transplantation, gene editing, or cloning. They were captured from different parts of the world."

"Did these people know that they will likely to be sacrificed sooner or later?"

"They had an inclination, since many of their colleagues never returned from the camp once taken out. They served a great useful purpose for the laboratory. They were to be used as guinea pigs when a need arises."

"What about the ladies who were pregnant?"

"Newly pregnant women knew that they might have their live fetus taken out for germinal cells."

"All of them somehow came to know that their organs of liver, kidney, and heart may be removed if they match with a required recipient, who is paying big money for the organ."

"How about the mutants they had created out of genetic experiments?"

"On another side of the campus, they noticed various mutations of animals and humans resulting from the genetic manipulations and experimentations. Some of them had very horrific features. One creature had human-looking face and head, but it had a long body with short arms and legs. As a result, it had to walk on the four extremities, similar to animals. It could talk and think like humans, but it had to sit on its buttocks to eat with the help of two front extremities. When it moves, it needs to use all four extremities like a cow, a horse, or a tiger."

"That is interesting. Did they see other types of mutants?"

"They witnessed humans with one eye in the center of their forehead like the aliens from outer land, some other humans with very long nose, almost three times longer than normal humans, and some with very big ears, twice the normal size. Some of the absolutely normal-appearing humans were caged, since they were reported to be vicious and violent with tendency to murder anyone in front of them. Some others were blind, some others dumb, and some others with very poor mental capacity, with the mental acumen of a two-year-old baby."

"Did they see any good mutants at all?"

"On the good side, they also noticed highly intelligent and extremely smart individuals with high IQ who can act as human calculators or human computers."

"How long do they have to keep studying the products of genetic engineering?"

"All of these are side effects of gene editing. The scientists kept them alive to study their nature and behavior, hoping to create a superhuman someday. The only way to study the effect of gene editing was to follow up the results for a long period, sometimes for many years."

"Anything very unusual in their findings?"

"Another major finding there was unisex people. They had been gene-edited before birth to devoid them of all sexual organs and sexual features. None of them had either male or female organs. They did not have male or female features on their body or face. No breasts, no facial hair, no muscles. They had basic bodies, smooth and glowing. The bottom had opening for rectum and anus as usual toward the backside, but the opening for urination was just a pee hole in the front. It is the outer end of urethra that empties urine from the urinary bladder. The whole perineum was one smooth flat face with a tiny hole in the front for urination and bigger hole in the back between buttocks for defecation."

"If they are unisex and do not have any sexual organs, how do they procreate?"

"They have the ability to clone themselves at their will."

"How is it possible to incubate the cloned baby without a uterus?"

"They grow an external pouch—similar to a kangaroo's pouch—for a short duration when incubating the cloned newborn."

"Why would they create such unisex people? How would the society benefit from them?"

"They were just workers or soldiers for the society to do the mundane jobs. They did not have any sexual desires or associated issues. They will work without any distractions. There will be no sexual discrimination, no sexual harassment, and no sexual diseases."

"So it is like the bees and ants, I guess."

"Yes, you can see that feature in bees and ants. There are one or two queens, whose job is to reproduce. Most of the inmates are, however, just sexless workers, who focus on getting the job done in a harmonious way."

"So this gene experiments appear to be lifelong commitment."

"Research on gene editing and creating designer babies is a lifelong commitment. Effects of the genetic manipulations have to be followed until birth of the offspring of the offspring. Afterward, the offspring has to be studied for its entire life as to physical, mental, intellectual, and emotional stability and growth. They have to be kept caged or held in house arrest and constantly observed. Some of the gene-edited babies have birth defects. Sometimes such defects may be visible externally, and sometimes the internal defects will remain invisible."

"So the raid was preplanned?"

"The raid was preplanned and was held as a top secret. However, it was easy for the DWS officers to get wind of it. There were several countries involved, and there were so many ways to know what is going on. They were prepared to make it look like a surprise. They had already evacuated the top scientists, the brain of the center. Everything else can be negotiated afterward."

"Why was it necessary to conduct this type of raid?"

"It was a necessary attack to satisfy certain member nations, since some of their key leaders had been assassinated through the DWS. There was a need to show an action against terrorism to satisfy the media. It was a tactic. Every country and every organization in the world want their dirty work done by some outsider from time to time. DWS served an important function for all, and it will always be there in some dormant fashion or other. Money and help come from all quarters when the need arises. However, they also started feeling that DWS had become too powerful and sometimes a threat to their own safety. The nations wanted to punish and protect DWS at the same time."

"So this was an eyewash episode?"

"This raid was to affect only a periphery of the enterprise and only for a short time. All the attacking nations would stop their attacks on the island immediately after the raid. That is when the World Genetic Research Laboratory will rebuild and restart functioning as before. All the employees and scientists would be released after questioning by this time, since there would be no proof of any illegal activity on their part. The fault is with the owners, whom they are still tracking down."

"Which were the countries that participated in the raid?"

"Investigators consisting of military personnel, scientists, researchers, sociologists, and biochemistry professors descended onto the island in a coordinated action plan under the leadership of the United States, with participation by China and Russia, along with representatives from European Union nations."

"I assume they learned something from the raid?"

"Their goal was not to stop the work of the laboratory but to study the work that has been done so far and to learn further. Instead of destroying everything, they wanted to preserve the work that had been done so far because it takes years of effort to reach this level of progress. They wanted to learn the good and bad of the outcome from this establishment. They know that science cannot be stopped and knowledge cannot be restricted and similar efforts will continue in the future because human curiosity is unstoppable."

"Did they find the new virus they were working on?"

THE CLINIC

"The laboratory has been working on creating a virus as the first step in creating life. Viruses have only RNA and do not need a full complex of DNA and do not need a full cell. They were able to put together the required chemicals in various setups and incubate them, hoping for their growth and multiplication. It was extremely important to keep them contained, since no one knew the effects of these viruses in the human body if they invade into one. Security and safety-keeping the new virus strains contained was given due attention and importance. Still, there was a suspected leak.

There was a theory promoted by certain high government officials that COVID-19 virus initially escaped from a virology laboratory in Wuhan by accident and that China had covered it up. Some others even went to the extreme to state that it was an intentional biological warfare initiated by China to dislodge the world economic order and to establish Chinese supremacy. They quoted the fact that the virus did not spread to Beijing or Shanghai or other parts of China but caused havoc to Europe, US, and certain other countries."

"Did they learn anything new about DNA?"

"The world's oldest DNA is traced to 1.2 million years ago from molars taken from mammoths. Each cell in the human body has six-foot length of DNA. Humans have 22,300 genes. Yeast has 6,000. Bacteria have 901. Lowest number in a bacterium is 473. Humans evolved and descended from common ancestor of apes. A 2007 study shows humans and rhesus monkeys share 93 percent of the same DNAs."

"What does the future of the world and that of humans look like?"

"All species, including humans, are going to be extinct someday. History proves it to be so. According to J. Richard Gott, there is a 95-percent probability that humans will be extinct in 7.8 million years from now. With climate change, global warming, and sea level rising, humans may have to learn to live underwater or in underwater cities in the future. Planet Earth will disappear in 7.5 billion years from now when the Sun becomes a red solar system and implodes on itself. It is postulated that aliens, who will be interested in studying human DNA and recreate the same, will inhabit Earth."

"Do they have any plans to save humanity?"

"The raid also unveiled a detailed plan to preserve human race in case of a manmade or natural catastrophe. The investigators were astounded to see a large underground storage area where many different items were deep-frozen in secure and sealed containers. They found pieces of skin, muscle, bone, brain, heart, ova, and sperms well preserved, which can be thawed in the future if a need arises. Intention of the scientists is to preserve humanity, since their extinction is certain to happen."

"What are other causes for such a major calamity?"

"The events in consideration were a nuclear war between nations when most of the world becomes uninhabitable. This island being away from other countries is unlikely to be contaminated. Another possibility was a meteorite or a broken piece of another planet colliding with Earth and aliens entering Earth."

"So what do they have in mind as possible plans?"

"They understand that genetic research has associated unpredictability as well as untoward side effects. Artificial intelligences and robotics will be widely used in genetic research. They know that the future of humanity depends on genetic manipulations and that women are best equipped than men to save the future. The world depends on women much more than men.

"There are particles smaller than atom—quark, gluons, preons, and muons. These may change our understanding of the universe. We need to plan for the future. Otherwise, humanity as we know will disappear from the face of earth, similar to the fate of dinosaurs, mammoths, and so many other extinct species."

"When do they resume work at the Lab Island again?"

"News of the raid will lose its value after a few days. Then the federal agents will leave the place as an uninhabitable, worthless place with no further use. Three months later, the work will resume at the World Genetic Research Laboratory with the same group of scientists and employees. It is a necessary evil for large corporations. Many countries want to keep it going. Their work and research must go on. DWS will continue its work. It is a necessity for the human race. Science cannot be stopped."

THE CLINIC

Everyone agreed with reluctance. Science must progress. The next leap in increasing longevity and improving health for humans is through genetic research and not by drugs. Survival of humanity depends on genetic technology.

Books Written by the Author

Venkit S. Iyer

venkitiyer.com

Dr. Venkit S. Iyer had studied and worked in the health-care field all his life; hence, his books are related to health care. All the books are available through Amazon.com.

- *Decision Making in Clinical Surgery* published by Jaypee Brothers medical publishers, New Delhi, India. It is a guidebook for medical students, residents, and interns and junior surgeons in clinical surgery. It is a symptom-based approach to common surgical problems as they encounter in the hospitals and their practice.
- *Aging well and Reaching Beyond* published by Evershine Press, Inc, Brandon, Florida, USA. It is for general reading for all with very useful information on preventive health care, wellness measures, elder-care issues, and end-of-life matters.
- *The Clinic* published by Page Publishing, Conneaut Lake, Pennsylvania, USA. It is based on genetic science, assisted reproductive technologies, and future of genetic therapy and written as a medical science fiction.

About the Author

Venkit S. Iyer was born in Palakkad District, Kerala state in India. His parents emphasized the value of education. This enabled him to achieve higher education and subsequent admission to medical college there. After completing his medical degree, he also did his post-graduation in surgery. Immediately afterward, he migrated to the United States of America for higher education and training in surgery. After completing internship and residency in New York, he started working at the same hospital as a full-time teaching faculty member in the department of surgery. After a year of work and teaching at the Albert Einstein College of Medicine, Bronx, New York, he decided to move to Florida to start a consulting private practice in general and vascular surgery. For the next thirty years, he practiced surgery at the same location in Palm Harbor, Florida, before subsequently retiring. Since then, he has participated in various medical missions and other charitable work.

Dr. Venkit S. Iyer is a board-certified surgeon, Fellow of the American College of Surgeons (FACS), Fellow of the Royal College of Physicians and Surgeons of Canada (FRCS-C), and Fellow of the International College of Surgeons (FICS), and holds a master's degree (MS) in surgery. He has held many leadership positions, teaching positions, and given many talks and lectures in various forums. He has authored three books so far and written numerous articles in various journals and magazines. They are listed in the previous page separately. His hobbies include tennis, golf, reading, and writing. For further information, please visit author's website: venkitiyer.com.

CPSIA information can be obtained
at www.ICGtesting.com
Printed in the USA
JSHW062005250822
29669JS00002B/11